'What have you
car?'

It wasn't a romantic
miss a beat at a voice from the past for Tessa
didn't recognise it as such.

The owner of the grey Volvo went on to say
with a sort of weary tolerance, 'You were
always under my feet before, and it looks as
if nothing's changed.'

Tessa looked up then, brown eyes wide and
startled. She'd been expecting to be the one
with the advantage. It hadn't occurred to her
that Ben Tarrant might have a long memory.

Abigail Gordon began writing some years ago at the suggestion of her sister, who is herself an established writer. She has found it an absorbing and fulfilling way of expressing herself, and feels that in the medical romance there is an opportunity to present realistically strong dramatic situations with which readers can identify. Abigail lives in a Cheshire village near Stockport, and is widowed with three grown-up sons and several grandchildren.

Recent titles by the same author:

A DAUNTING DIVERSION
CALMER WATERS
NO SHADOW OF DOUBT
JOEL'S WAY

TARRANT'S
PRACTICE

BY
ABIGAIL GORDON

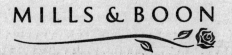

MILLS & BOON, the Rose Device and LOVE ON CALL are trademarks of the publisher.
Harlequin Mills & Boon Limited,
Eton House, 18–24 Paradise Road, Richmond, Surrey TW9 1SR
This edition published by arrangement with
Harlequin Enterprises B.V.

© Abigail Gordon 1995

ISBN 0 263 79098 3

Set in 10 on 11½ pt Linotron Times
03-9507-56065

Typeset in Great Britain by CentraCet, Cambridge
Made and printed in Great Britain

CHAPTER ONE

TESSA'S eyes raked the crowded platform as she wrestled her case off the train. The other half of her family had promised to meet her, but her young brother, Dominic, was notoriously casual about arrangements, and to find him waiting would be a pleasant surprise.

He wasn't, and as the InterCity service eased itself smoothly out of the station, taking most of those who'd been on the platform with it, Tessa looked around her.

A young porter, eyeing the slim figure in a black cloak and leggings, asked, 'Need any help, miss?' and was rewarded with a bright smile from beneath a pink felt hat with a turned-back brim.

'No, thanks,' she told him. 'I was expecting someone to meet me, but he hasn't turned up, by the looks of it.'

'Must be crazy,' he said with a cheeky grin. 'Catch me standing you up!'

You'd have to be given the chance first, boyo, Tessa thought, as she told him pleasantly, 'We're talking about my brother.'

As if on cue a breezy voice called from behind, 'Hi, Doc,' and Tessa swung round to find a youth with the same thick brown locks and fair skin as herself strolling along the platform towards her.

'Dominic!' she cried, giving him a rapturous hug. 'So you didn't forget.'

'Of course I didn't,' he said, as the porter moved away reluctantly. He was squirming out of her embrace

5

and looking around him. 'Easy on, Tess!' he protested. 'Some of my mates might be around.'

She drew back laughingly.

'If past vibes are anything to go by, I'd have thought that most of your friends would be envious to see you getting a hug from me. *They* wouldn't push me away. I well remember them queueing up to have their phoney complaints examined.'

He'd picked up her case and was making a pretence of collapsing under its weight.

'You couldn't blame them for that,' he parried jokingly. 'You were always ready for the chance to practise on us.'

He led the way on to the station forecourt and deposited her case into the boot of a Mini that had been sprayed in psychedelic colours. Shading her eyes from its glare, Tessa tucked herself in beside him and they were off.

'When is your appointment?' Dominic asked as they chugged along.

'Tomorrow afternoon at two-thirty is when I shall hopefully make my impact on the partners of Woodbank Surgery.'

'You fancy being a GP, then?' he said as he negotiated the turning on to the drive of a small block of flats.

'Yes, I do, but my interview tomorrow is only for twelve months' training in the practice. At the end of it I can either go back to a hospital job, or, if there is a permanent vacancy available in their practice or any other, take that. So you see it's one step at a time, dear brother.'

She eyed the carefree young face beside her. 'And what about you? How is your life progressing?'

'Not bad,' he told her airily. 'In and between selling

properties I manage to do the rounds of the local social scene, and keep the bank manager at bay. . .just.'

He was unlocking the front door of the nearest of the ground-floor flats and, as she followed him inside, Tessa grimaced.

'I can see one thing that you're *not* doing.'

'What's that?' he asked warily.

'Using a vac and duster. The place looks as if it hasn't been touched since my last visit.'

She moved into the kitchen and he followed, waiting for her reaction.

'Ah! Conscience pricked you, eh, me boy? Looks as if you've actually been using elbow grease and hot water in here. Well done!'

'Wait until you see the bathroom,' he told her with casual pride. 'You can actually see your face in the morror.'

Tessa eyed him in mock surprise. 'You don't say! And there aren't any spiders in the bath?'

'Not living ones, anyway.'

While she was unpacking, Dominic went to get them a Chinese take-away, and, as she hung up her clothes in the ramshackle wardrobe in the flat's spare bedroom, Tessa was thinking that they were both free spirits, Dominic and herself, but at twenty-six years old, and with eight years in medicine under her belt, she sometimes felt her three years' seniority to be thirty-three when she observed her brother's lifestyle.

However, she rarely criticised, as she was no conformist herself. Her colleagues in medical school and the London hospital where she'd spent the last three years, knew her to be a confident, uncomplicated young woman, who spoke her mind, was always ready for some fun if there was any to be had. . .and wore whatever happened to be in fashion when off duty.

They also knew her to be a good doctor, and tomorrow Tessa was taking the first step towards a new facet of her career—general practice. She'd come down from London to be interviewed for the position of trainee at the surgery where a lifetime ago she and her family had been patients.

That had been during the time when, first, her father had been treated by the doctors there for a heart condition that had taken him from them in his early forties, and secondly, it had been her mother's turn, three years later, to be attended by the doctors of the Woodbank practice, when she was seriously injured in a car crash, which eventually brought about her death.

When the two teenagers had found themselves parent-less they had reacted in different ways. Dominic had become difficult and lazy, falling behind in his school work, while Tessa had discovered two things. One was that she'd seen enough of suffering to make her want to help combat it, and the other, connected with the first, was that she was in love with Benjamin Tarrant, the tall fair-haired GP who had attended her mother.

To a bright-faced, bouncy teenager with a mane of long brown hair, it had all seemed perfectly simple. She loved Ben Tarrant, so naturally he must feel the same.

At the time of her youthful passion he had been the junior partner in the busy Woodbank practice, a serious young man with straight blond hair, a finely chiselled face, and bright blue eyes, in which Tessa had been sure she saw a passion to match her own.

When he was due to visit the house she would move heaven and earth to be there, even if it meant being late for school or finishing early, and her Aunt Joan, who had taken over the reins of the household, would tut disapprovingly at her niece's blatant pursuit of the young doctor.

If Ben Tarrant had seen her adoration, he'd given no sign. In those days he'd been grave and preoccupied and obviously unaware of his attractiveness, yet it hadn't stopped her from dreaming of him waiting at the altar for her as she floated along in a beautiful wedding-dress.

When a school friend had told her that he was engaged to a stunning redhead she'd refused to believe it at first, but after having seen them together and observed his absorption in his very beautiful companion, Tessa had almost changed her career plans from medical school to convent.

But the urge to join the medical fraternity had been strong, and at eighteen she'd gone to college, leaving a more mature Dominic behind with Aunt Joan, and, among an assortment of students of her own age, her hopeless passion for Ben Tarrant had seemed to be of less importance, and she'd felt rather foolish for bombarding him with make-believe illnesses.

Absorbed in his own moods and misery at that time, Dominic hadn't been aware of her youthful crush, and she'd never enlightened him since, for which she was thankful, as her young brother would no doubt have something highly amusing to say if he knew that one of the GPs who were to interview her tomorrow was the object of her unrequited passion from long ago.

She could laugh at it now, and if Ben Tarrant was still as heart-stopping, so what? She'd had a few men friends during her years at university and while training in hospital, and knew that this time she would be meeting him on a more equal footing.

Tessa was hoping that he wouldn't recognise her.

Let's face it, she told herself with a smile as she put the last of her clothes away, he barely noticed you then, so it isn't likely that he'll remember you after all this time, and if he does, what does it matter? If he takes you on *he'll* be the lucky one. You're fresh, fit, and fancy-free. The odds are that Ben Tarrant and his copper-haired fiancée will have a house full of little Tarrants by now.

A year in general practice would be the final part of her training and she was looking forward to it. While searching through the lists of practices looking for trainees, she'd seen Woodbank amoung them, and had seen the chance to go back to the Midlands for a while to be near Dominic and her old haunts. The fact that the practice was one of them had a lot to do with her decision.

Dominic had jumped at the idea of her coming to live with him for two reasons: the first that he was very fond of 'Doc', as he called her, and the second that her sharing the flat would help his finances. Aunt Joan had gone back to her cottage in Cornwall once he was settled in a place of his own and, though he liked his freedom, Dominic wasn't the world's expert at making ends meets.

He was downstairs now, yelling that the 'flied lice' had arrived, and as she went to join him Tessa knew that she wanted this year's training in her old home town, wanted it a lot.

Her appointment with the doctors at Woodbank wasn't until the early afternoon, between surgeries, and when Dominic, looking reasonably spruce for a trainee valuer, popped his head around the bedroom door at eight-thirty the next morning, she opened a sleepy eye.

He hooted when he saw the clothes she'd laid out for the interview—a neat beige tweed suit with a tan open-necked blouse, and bronze lace-up shoes.

'I was about to ask how the twentieth-century version of Dr Finlay is this morning, but you're going to look more like Janet in that outfit!'

Tessa slung a pillow at him.

'Begone, callow youth! I'm out to make an impression, and much as I love my black cloak——'

'You don't want to be mistaken for Batwoman or the wicked witch?' he finished for her, as his head disappeared and his feet clattered down the stairs.

'Not until I've convinced medics Brown, Tarrant and Patel that I'm just what the doctors ordered,' she called after him from the landing and, as the front door slammed, Tessa admitted to herself that it had felt strange saying the name that long ago had been forever on her lips.

After a leisurely soak in Dominic's Spartan bathroom she went downstairs to forage for breakfast, but gave up after finding only a shrivelled orange and half a sliced loaf that had a green film on it.

Big breakfasts weren't in her line, but neither was no breakfast, especially when she needed her wits about her, and so, with her long brown hair still in damp tendrils, she flung on a pair of jeans and a red cotton shirt and sprinted to the shops across from the flats.

Within minutes she was returning with fresh bread, cereals, and two bottles of milk clutched in her arms. On the edge of the pavement, waiting to cross, she was startled as a young child in a push-chair let out a fretful screech, and one of the bottles of milk slipped out of her arms and landed on the bonnet of a grey Volvo parked at the pavement beside her.

Tessa gave a dismayed gasp and reached out to grab it, but before she could do so it had rolled off and, bouncing on the mudguard, landed on the road where

the glass broke and the milk began to spread in a white
tide.

She groaned. If the driver of the car approached
from the rear he wouldn't see it, and the moment he
moved off his tyres would be on the glass. She looked
around her. He must be in one of the shops. There was
a newsagent's nearby—maybe he'd gone to buy a
paper. She hoped he hadn't seen the bottle hit the
bonnet and mudguard of his car, and, as she peered
anxiously at the bodywork, a voice said in cold enquiry,
'What's going on here, then? What have you been
doing to my car?'

It wasn't a romantic moment. Her heart didn't miss
a beat at a voice from the past. Tessa didn't recognise
it as such, as she was carefully picking up the broken
glass, anxious to atone for her carelessness, and thinking that if she crouched in the gutter long enough he
might back the car away and drive off.

The owner of the grey Volvo went on to say with a
sort of weary tolerance, 'You were always under my
feet before, and it looks as if nothing's changed.'

She looked up then, brown eyes wide and startled.
She'd been expecting to be the one with the advantage.
It hadn't occurred to her that Ben Tarrant might have
a long memory. It was amazing that he'd recognised
her, considering that he'd barely looked in her direction all those years ago.

He seemed taller and broader, but the straight fair
sheen of his hair was the same, and the bright blue
eyes, in a face that had never really faded from her
mind.

Tessa straightened up from her crouching position
and, with her confidence returning, raised herself to
her full height, which brought her level with the top
button of his smart navy jacket.

'I'm surprised that you remembered me, Dr Tarrant,' she said, hiding her gratification at the fact.

'I didn't. Not your face anyway. When you applied for the position of trainee at the surgery your name seemed familiar, and on checking our records I saw that your family had once been patients at Woodbank. The address you gave was in the flats opposite, and I was on my way to explain that due to something unforeseen we are going to have to put your interview back by half an hour. I'd just parked and was about to call on you when I saw you come out of the flat and cross the road to the shops, and decided to make a call on a nearby patient while you were so engaged.'

'I see,' she said slowly. So much for that. The remembering had all been on her part, but not quite. He obviously hadn't forgotten that she'd been a pest! Well, Benjamin Tarrant was about to see the new Tessa Martin, cool, competent, and a far cry from the teenage would-be seductress—that was, if she was offered the post.

'Thanks for taking the trouble to let me know about the new time for my appointment,' she said breezily, 'and now, if you'll excuse me, I'll go and have my breakfast.'

'You've spilt your milk,' he pointed out.

'Yes, I know, and I'm sorry your car got involved, but I still have a bottle left, so. . .'

He'd opened the car door and was sliding behind the steering-wheel, and, his bright blue gaze giving nothing away, he told her, 'Enjoy your breakfast. If we take you on at Woodbank you'll be already knee-deep in patients by this time of the morning,' and on that bland note of warning he drove off.

* * *

The Woodbank practice was housed in a building of
smooth Accrington brick within a courtyard off the
main street of the Midlands market town where Tessa
had been brought up, and, as she stood outside its solid
remembered façade at the revised appointment time,
she was wishing that there hadn't been the messy
episode with Ben Tarrant earlier.

Her intention was to present a smart, confident
image to the three partners, Ben in particular, if only
to show him that her adolescent yearnings had gone,
and that he was observing a competent young doctor
who would be an asset to the practice. She straightened
her slim shoulders.

Nothing has changed, she told herself firmly. Go in
and forget that you dropped a bottle of milk on to his
smart grey car, and that your re-introduction after
eight years was at gutter level. All right, he remembered you. So what? It was only as a name in patient
records, not, thankfully, as the teenage temptress who
dogged his steps, so be glad that the only thing you
have to prove is that you know the job.

'So you're the young lady who was one of our
patients in time past,' Hugo Brown, the elderly senior
partner of the practice, said when she was shown into
a new office suite at the back of the building.

He was seated behind a big polished table with
Benjamin Tarrant on one side and a smiling, dark-
skinned man on the other. Tessa smiled back. He was
the only one of the trio giving out any warmth. Ben
Tarrant was observing her gravely, blue eyes giving
nothing away, and Hugo Brown, after his initial greeting, had delved into his coat pocket and brought out a
large white handkerchief into which he was blowing his
nose loudly.

Dr Brown had seemed old to her eight years ago,

and she would have expected him to be long gone, but it was obviously not the case. He was a small man, with bushy white hair, a hollow, cadaverous face, and wise old eyes that she recollected could reflect benevolence or sparking fire according to the climate of the occasion.

The third member of the trio was obviously Dr Ranjit Patel, who must have become a partner of the Woodbank practice during her absence, and who at this moment seemed to be giving off the least daunting vibes.

'Yes,' she agreed smilingly into the silence that was waiting for her to speak. 'Until going to medical school I lived in this area, and all of my family were patients here.'

'And now?' the elderly doctor asked.

Tessa's smile didn't wilt.

'My parents died within a short time of each other, and of recent years it will have been only my brother and my aunt who have been on your lists, but as both of them enjoy excellent health I doubt that you will have seen much of them.'

Ben Tarrant had given his elderly colleague a wary glance as he'd questioned her, and Tessa wondered why Hugo Brown wasn't aware of the deaths of her parents and their subsequent deletion from the surgery records but, as she pondered the fact, Ben Tarrant was saying smoothly, 'Yes, we're aware that your aunt and brother are patients of ours, although I believe the lady has now left the district.'

Tessa eyed him thoughtfully. Was this his way of letting her know that *he* wasn't asleep? Unless he'd changed drastically, she didn't need to be told that. Her passion for him hadn't blinded her to the fact that he was an excellent doctor, tireless, painstaking, and very knowledgeable when it came to his profession.

'Yes, that is so,' she confirmed, controlling the urge to prod the interview into life. She needn't have concerned herself. It seemed that Ben Tarrant had the matter in hand.

'Shall I take over, Hugo?' he said.

'Aye,' the other agreed. 'Whatever you decide it won't have that much effect on me,' and, placing the fingertips of both hands together in a church roof-like position, he rested his chin on them and gazed up at the ceiling.

For the first time since she'd entered the room, Ben Tarrant smiled. It softened the lean lines of his face and momentarily wiped off the gravity, and Tessa began to feel less on the defensive.

As they faced each other, a blade of autumn sunlight came through the window, gleaming on the straight gold pelt of his hair, and as Tessa's eyes went over the three men opposite she thought that here were gold, silver, and bronze. . .and she was the challenger, skilled and ready to show her worth, even if it was only for twelve months' training.

'If you come to practise here with us at Woodbank you will work with myself mostly,' Ben Tarrant was explaining. 'I am the trainer, and you will be guided by me in all aspects of the practice. I have gone through all the necessary procedures to qualify me to do this, and would expect us to have a good *working* relationship.'

Had she imagined the emphasis on the word? she wondered, her eyes on the firm lines of the mouth that once she had ached to feel on hers. Was there a warning that a working relationship was all that would be on offer? If so, that was fine by her.

'I will outline the functions of the practice and what your role would be in it,' he was continuing, 'and then if you have any questions for us we'll be only too happy to answer them. All right?'

'Yes, of course,' she said calmly. She did have questions to ask, but it would appear that first she would have some to answer, as he was telling her.

'However, before we start discussing Woodbank, tell us about yourself, Dr Martin. We are aware of the places where you have trained, but would like to hear what area of medical care you have specialised in during that time.'

Tessa's smile was carefree. She was on safe ground there. She'd enjoyed the last three years. They'd been hard and challenging, but she'd taken to hospital life like a duck to water.

'I spent my first year in hospital training, half on the wards and half in Theatre,' she told them. 'My second and third were split into four areas: paediatrics, obstetrics, gynaecology and, at the other end of the scale, geriatrics.'

'And which of them did you enjoy the most?' Dr Patel asked softly.

Tessa gave him a bright, confident beam.

'Paediatrics. I enjoyed them all, but health care for children really interested me.'

'So we can rely on passing all the noisy little monsters on to you, then,' Hugo Brown said with a dry laugh.

Tessa smiled in response, restraining the urge to tell him that really sick children are rarely noisy.

Ben Tarrant was taking over again.

'I take it that you're aware of the differences between hospital life and general practice?'

'Er—yes. I think so.'

'The pressures can be very great on a GP you know.'

No worse than twelve-hour, or even longer, stints on the wards, she thought.

'And there is always the thing that one isn't prepared for cropping up.'

Was he trying to dissuade her?

She nodded.

'Yes, I expect that, but you would be there on those occasions?'

'Oh, yes, I'll be on hand—we all will, except that Dr Brown will be retiring shortly before your twelve months is up.'

So the old man was due to go, and then what? A new partner? That could work out just right for herself. . .if she fitted in with the doctors. . .and patients. If she decided that general practice was for her.

Ben Tarrant began to explain how the practice was run, the financing of it, staffing levels, the appointments system, visiting arrangements, and as Tessa took it all in a wave of enthusiasm swept over her.

When she'd seen the vacancy advertised in the *British Medical Journal* the idea of coming back to her old haunts as a GP had appealed to her, but she hadn't realised just how much, until the interview had commenced.

When he'd finished explaining, Ben Tarrant sat back in his chair and said, 'Now it's your turn—fire away.'

She did.

'Do you perform minor surgery here?'

'Yes, we do, as long as we see no risk to the patient.'

'How long will I be allowed to spend with each patient in the consulting-room?'

'Depends on how many's waiting,' Hugo Brown told her with his dry chuckle.

Ben Tarrant shook his head.

'No, that's not the case. For the first few weeks we'll

allow you ten minutes, give or take a few seconds, and after that seven, but don't worry about that. Some consultations take longer, and some are shorter. They usually balance themselves out, but that is roughly the amount of time you will be allocated.'

'Will I be allowed one day off each week for further training?' she asked.

'Yes, of course,' he replied. 'The course you will attend is run, as I'm sure you're aware, by the General Practice Section of the Department of Postgraduate Medicine and Dentistry. I have all the details.'

Tessa had another question.

'You have explained that the practice is not fund-holding, and I'm presuming that it is because it has less than ten thousand patients.'

He nodded. 'That is so.'

'If the number of patients did exceed that number, would you consider changing to a fund-holding system?'

Hugo Brown tutted impatiently at the question, but Dr Patel inclined his head in acknowledgement of it, and Ben Tarrant said equably, 'Possibly, but it's a question that doesn't arise at this moment. Should our patients increase enough to give us the opportunity to diversify, then it would be something to which we would have to give very serious thought.'

And so it had proceeded, with Ben Tarrant holding the floor, with the occasional caustic comment from his elderly partner, and Dr Patel making soft-voiced observations when he thought fit.

When the interview eventually came to a close, Tessa had become aware that Dr Brown wasn't bothered one way or the other whether she joined them, that Ranjit Patel appeared to feel exactly opposite, and as for Ben Tarrant . . . He'd been polite and helpful, but each time their glances had held she'd been conscious that his eyes were veiled, and his mouth, though not exactly forbidding, wasn't smiling like that of his dark-skinned colleague. She had a feeling that there was disapproval in the air.

'Are you due back in London soon?' he asked, as they got to their feet.

'I'm here for three days,' Tessa told him, rising to her fullest height in the respectable suit and the neat flat shoes, and still only reaching his breast-bone.

'Fine,' he said crisply. 'We shall have a discussion once you've gone and will be in touch. I'd like to give you our decision before you go back down south. That way you won't be left wondering whether to explore any other avenues. Or have you done that already?'

'No,' she told him with her habitual candour. 'Not yet. I wanted to see how things turned out here first.'

'So you really do want to join us?'

Tessa's beautiful dark eyes were serious.

'Yes, I do. I was brought up around here. My young brother of whom I'm very fond still lives in the area, and what is more. . .'

'Yes?' he questioned, as the end of her sentence hung in the air.

'Er—it was nothing,' she mumbled.

It had been on the tip of her tongue to tell him that curiosity could have had something to do with it as well, finding out what he'd been up to in the last eight years, and how the glamorous redhead was shaping up.

The following afternoon, after giving Dominic's flat a spring clean, Tessa was outside, shining the windows as her final chore. Dressed in an old sweatshirt of her brother's and a pair of torn jeans, she was feeling hot and grubby, and the next item on her list was going to be a long hot soak.

When her name was called from below, she swivelled round on the ladder and found herself looking into Ben Tarrant's eyes.

'Oh! It's you,' she said uncomfortably, wishing that Dominic's sweater wasn't so tatty, and the jeans torn in a less conspicuous place.

'I can see that you're busy,' he said, 'and I don't want to interrupt, but I thought you'd like to know that we've made a decision.'

Tessa brushed a strand of damp hair off her brow with a grimy hand.

'Yes, I would. . .very much.' She began to descend the ladder. 'Would you like to come inside?'

'No.' He put out his hand to halt her. 'I'm pushed for time, and you're busy. What I have to say can be said in a matter of seconds.'

Her spirits plummeted. That didn't sound very promising.

'We'd like you to join us, Dr Martin. What do you say?'

Her bright beam flashed out.

'I say. . .yes, please, Dr Tarrant.'

His smile was less exuberant than hers, but he was making the effort.

'That's good. We'll confirm it in writing, of course, and sort out a date for you to start.' He paused, and Tessa wondered what was coming next. She was about to be surprised. 'Perhaps you'd like to come for a drink this evening to cement the arrangement?'

Tessa stared at him. At seventeen she would have leapt at it, at almost twenty-seven she was more cautious, but the idea wasn't without its appeal.

'You mean with the three of you?'

'No, just me, I'm afraid. The little Patels will be eagerly awaiting Ranjit's return after evening surgery, and Dr and Mrs Brown don't move far in the evenings.'

'And won't your family be waiting for you?'

She supposed she'd a nerve questioning a harmless invitation to go for a drink, but he was the one who'd brought family matters into it.

He was straight-faced now, but his next words told her that the glint in his eyes was amusement.

'My parents have long since stopped monitoring my movements.'

'Your parents?' she asked, aware that surprise was making her voice squeak.

'Yes. I live with my mother and father. Does that surprise you?'

'No, of course not,' she fibbed.

'I used to have a place of my own, but when my father became quite ill I gave it up and moved back home, as my mother couldn't cope alone.'

'So you're not married?'

He eyed her curiously.

'Why do you ask?'

'I seem to remember that you were engaged at the time you treated my mother.'

His mouth tightened.

'You remember rightly, and you haven't answered my question.'

'Yes, I'd love to come for a drink,' she told him buoyantly. 'I've had my fill of Dominic's cobwebs.'

'I'll pick you up after evening surgery. Eight o'clock, say?'

'Yes, that'll be fine,' she told him, and on that agreement he went on his way, leaving her to marvel that such a presentable man was still unattached.

* * *

Alfredo's Wine Bar was crowded and, as Tessa watched Ben Tarrant waiting his turn at the bar, she was observing the rest of the customers at the same time. It was obviously one of the 'in' places, judging from the cosmopolitan clientele who were packing themselves in, and she found herself thinking it strange that he'd chosen this place.

She would have expected the reticent, flaxen-haired GP to have frequented somewhere more select, but if the greeting he'd received from Alfredo was anything to go by, Ben Tarrant was a regular customer.

For her part, the place suited her fine. There'd been lots of places like this near the London hospital where she'd been based, and often a gang of them would meet in the noisy, smoky, but convivial atmosphere to relax after a hard day on the wards or in Theatre.

After her far from fashionable outfit of the afternoon, Tessa had gone through her wardrobe to find something that looked less Oxfam-orientated, and had come up with a close-fitting white beaded jumper and a long black skirt that flared above pointed ankle boots of the same colour.

She'd passed over the cherished black cape and the pink hat, and put a short black jacket over the jumper, having an instinctive feeling that they wouldn't go down too well with the man who was to be her trainer. All right, his opinion wasn't all that important, not about what she wore, anyway, but as she'd only just been offered the chance to become part of the practice he belonged to, it wouldn't do to appear too nonconformist at the outset.

'At last,' he breathed, as he appeared beside her with a bottle of dry white wine and two glasses. 'It's always busy in here, but not usually as crowded as this.'

He pointed to where the proprietor, a small dark man, was bustling to and fro.

'Alfredo Conti is a patient of ours. His heart is less healthy than it should be, but he won't rest. His wife is quite capable of taking over, but he won't hear of it. One of these days. . .'

Even as he was speaking there was a commotion near the bar, and within seconds a group had formed around an inert figure on the floor.

'Stand back, give him some air,' somebody called, and immediately Ben Tarrant was on his feet. He grabbed her hand.

'Come on, Tessa, it sounds as if we might be needed,' and he began to elbow his way through the crowd.

It wasn't the little Italian on the floor as they'd half expected. It was a much younger man and he was deathly pale.

Ben Tarrant released her hand and, bending over the limp figure, he said briskly, 'Stand back everyone, please. We're doctors. We'll take over,' and as Tessa went to kneel beside him there was a strong feeling inside her that she really had come home.

CHAPTER TWO

'You'll be the new trainee, I expect,' a voice said from behind as Tessa rang the bell at the back entrance to the Woodbank practice on her first morning.

She swung round to find a tall grey-haired woman observing her with smiling interest.

'Yes, I am. Tessa Martin's the name,' she said, holding out her hand.

'Jean Carswell,' the other woman said as they shook hands. 'Dr Patel's receptionist.' She produced a key out of her pocket. 'It looks as if we're the first to arrive. Mind you, it's only just gone eight. We don't get the show off the road until half-past.'

As the door swung open she led the way into a small kitchen nearby and immediately went to fill the kettle.

'Hope you'll be happy here with us, Tessa,' she said over her shoulder. 'Most of the staff here are great.'

'How many are there?' she asked.

'Three receptionists—each doctor has his own. Gaynor Banks does the necessary for Dr Brown, and Anne-Marie Davies watches over Dr Tarrant. Then there's Alice Shepherd, the practice nurse, Polly, the cleaner, who'll be somewhere on the premises, and various other folk who come and go on a part-time basis.'

Tessa nodded.

'You've had other trainees previously, I take it?'

'One or two,' Jean said, with a wry smile.

'And did they settle in all right?'

25

'Some did. . .some didn't, and I'm afraid there's been more that didn't than did.'

'Why is that, do you think?' Tessa asked, undeterred.

'Hard to say. It's something you'll discover for yourself, I reckon, but if you don't, it won't be any fault of Dr Tarrant's. They don't come any better.'

Footsteps in the passage outside announced other arrivals, and as Tessa turned to face them three more female members of staff came into the kitchen. When they saw the newcomer there was silence for a second, and she stepped forward.

'I'm Tessa Martin. I'm to be here for twelve months as a trainee GP.'

The woman nearest to her, a smooth-faced brunette in her thirties, exclaimed, 'Of course! It had slipped my mind that you were joining us today. I'm Alice Shepherd, the practice nurse, as must be apparent from the way I'm dressed. Nice to meet you.'

'And I'm Gaynor Banks,' the fluffy-haired blonde next to her said with a nervous giggle. 'Dr Brown's receptionist.'

The third member of the trio was a tall, slim girl of about Tessa's age, with crisp black curls in a short, stylish cut, and an attractive face that was spoiled by its tightness. It was her eyes that Tessa noticed the most. They were cold and antagonistic.

'I'm Anne-Marie Davies,' she said in a voice that matched her looks. 'Dr Tarrant's receptionist, and woe betide anyone who brings him aggro.'

Tessa eyed steel with steel. What sort of a welcome was this? she thought angrily.

'What a unique way you have of introducing yourself,' she commented with smooth irony, and Jean

Carswell, who was pouring tea into white china mugs, smothered a laugh.

The outside door opened and shut, and Ben Tarrant's cold-eyed protectress swivelled round as if someone had pulled a string. When he appeared in the doorway in a gleaming white shirt and a dark suit, with a lightweight raincoat thrown over the top, her manner softened, and Tessa thought that although he might not have found his Cinderella, she'd like to bet that Anne-Marie was only waiting to be invited to the ball. . .if she hadn't been already.

But his eyes were on herself, flicking over her quickly, taking in the nut-brown hair, tied neatly back, and the cream silk blouse and brown checked skirt, the neat tie shoes on her feet, and the bright eyes that were waiting to hear what he had to say.

'Ah, so you've arrived, Dr Martin,' he said smoothly.

'Have you been introduced to everyone?'

'Of those present. . .yes,' she replied.

'Good, then perhaps you'd like to come with me and I'll explain the routine that I intend us to adopt primarily.

'Your consulting-room will be the small one next to this,' he said, as he took her into a medium-sized room with all the trappings of a busy GP in it. 'I think it advisable that you should sit in on my consultations for a while, before facing the patients on your own. It will help you to gauge timing and give you a general idea of our approach.'

Tessa stifled a sigh. Did he think she wasn't used to dealing with the general public? She'd been embroiled in more outpatients' clinics than she'd had hot dinners, but he was eyeing her coolly, and something told her it wasn't the moment to start blowing her own trumpet.

Time enough when she'd proved herself an asset to the practice.

She hadn't seen anything of Ben Tarrant since the night he'd taken her to Alfredo's and they'd found themselves dealing with a generalised epileptic seizure, but she'd thought about him a lot—too much, in fact— and she'd told herself on more than one occasion that her only interest in him was as a future colleague, that he was too quiet and morose for someone like herself, and each time she'd said it she'd believed it. . .almost.

They'd taken the youth home in Ben's car and, after having deposited him with his surprised and distressed parents, Ben had suggested to them that their son attend the surgery the following day for a consultation.

'It might have been due solely to the bug that he's been fighting off,' Ben had told them reassuringly when they'd stressed that there'd never been any epilepsy in the family, 'but an attack of that nature needs to be followed up.' He'd sized up the patient, who was obviously feeling confused and disorientated, and said, 'I'll see you tomorrow then, young man?' and been rewarded with a reluctant nod.

As he'd driven Tessa home Ben had said wryly, 'So much for our quiet drink.'

'I wouldn't call Alfredo's quiet,' she'd said laughingly.

He'd frowned.

'You didn't care for the place?'

'I didn't say that. As a matter of fact, it was just the kind of place I like, plenty of noise and bustle.'

His face had cleared as he'd told her, 'I go in there because it's convenient if I want to unwind, and because I like Alfredo. He's a stubborn little blighter, and it wouldn't have surprised me if it had been he who'd collapsed, but I have to admire the way he puts everything he's got into the business.'

When they'd stopped outside Dominic's flat in the golden autumn dusk it had still been early, and she'd asked him in for a drink. The day that had started off with a host of mundane chores had improved as it went on. She'd been offered a year at the Woodbank practice and renewed her acquaintance with her youthful Prince Charming who, surprisingly, hadn't found his Cinderella, and it had occurred to her that it might be the reason why he was so reticent and non-committal.

She'd noticed that he'd soon changed the subject when she'd mentioned his beautiful ex-fiancée, but surely if that relationship had foundered there would have been others? He was too attractive for there not to have been.

'No, thanks,' he'd said to the offer of the drink. 'I'll get off home and see how my folks are coping.'

She'd nodded, feeling oddly deflated, and she wasn't sure whether it was because he'd refused the invitation, or because he still had his parents.

'I'll wait to hear from you, then,' she'd said.

'It will be in the next few days,' he'd told her, and as he'd walked back to his car at the pavement's edge and given her a casual wave as he got in, Tessa had wondered if he ever did anything crazy—ever lost his temper, got drunk, or made passionate love—or was he just a very attractive robot?

The moment surgery commenced she knew he was no robot, not in the consulting-room, anyway. As each patient came in he explained to them who she was, that Dr Martin was assisting in the practice, that she'd had varied hospital experience, and was now observing the role of the family doctor, and there were very few patients who questioned the fact. On the whole they gave the impression that, as long as they were seeing Dr Tarrant, it could be Mickey Mouse seated beside him, and for his part, apart from the occasional quiet word of explanation for her benefit, he listened carefully to what they had to say and then dealt with it in an efficient and forthright manner that had her amazed at his knowledge.

He seemed to know instinctively those who were in need of medical help, and those who thought they were, and he was equally considerate with both. Children and the elderly were treated with a calm gentleness that helped to remove apprehension without any let-up of his attention to their needs and, as the morning progressed with a parade of patients seeking medical care, Tessa realised that whatever Ben Tarrant might be out of the surgery, he was a human dynamo inside it.

At the commencement of the morning he'd donned a pair of rimless glasses which had made him look even more remote, and now, as the last patient closed the door behind them, he was eyeing her enquiringly through the lenses.

'Well?' he asked drily. 'Any questions?'

She wanted to tell him how much she admired his expertise, his knowledge and dedication, but it wasn't her style to flatter her superiors, and so she told him with a laugh, 'Piece of cake.'

The eyes behind the glasses were cold.

'You think so, eh? You're very confident, Dr Martin. . .and flippant about the profession we both belong to.'

Tessa felt her colour rise and, on the defensive now, she muttered, 'Maybe.'

'Yes, well, we'll see. I'll expect you back here at

four-thirty for evening surgery, and after you've had your lunch you can familiarise yourself with the lay-out of the practice and get to know the rest of the staff,' he said coldly.

As she sat in a café around the corner from the surgery, Tessa wished she could learn to keep her mouth shut. Why, when she was so full of admiration, had she gone out of her way to antagonise him?

Resolutely she switched her mind from those chilly moments in his consulting-room to the patients he'd treated that morning. They'd been an interesting bunch. There'd been the young executive, incredibly handsome, smartly dressed, with the inevitable brief-case and a meeting to attend after he'd seen his GP. He was slim and fine-boned, obviously no stranger to stress in the office, and had all the signs of a duodenal ulcer. Ben Tarrant had previously prescribed a course of Zantac, an ulcer-healing drug, but the patient had complained that where the painful acid attacks were often months apart, of late they had been more fre-quent, and being in a private medicine scheme he had asked to see a specialist.

It had been clear during the consultation that here were two men who could discuss the problem intelli-gently, and even though Ben had felt there to be no cause for urgency he had agreed to make an appoint-ment, as the patient had suffered with the problem for some years, and it wasn't getting any better.

'I would suggest your taking the Zantac for a longer period,' he'd told him, 'maybe six months, and see how it goes, but there's no harm in your having another opinion if you so desire.'

Then there had been the middle-aged housewife who some months previously had consulted him because of extreme lethargy and dryness of the skin and hair.

Blood-tests had shown her to be suffering from an underactive thyroid, and he had put her on permanent thyroxine. At the time she hadn't been too concerned about it, as she could remember her mother having a goitre as a child, and it not having seemed to bother her a great deal. Today, however, she had been very upset to discover that the deficiency could cause other health problems.

She had come in for the results of a blood-test taken the previous week to check on the state of the thyroid, and Ben had told her that the cholesterol in her blood was at a dangerously high level, and that she was anaemic, both factors being due to the underactive thyroid. Where she hadn't been alarmed when the original diagnosis was made, now she was upset to find that it wasn't all as simple as she'd first thought.

Ben had reassured her that although it had caused other problems they in turn were not life-threatening if treated, and for the cholesterol he prescribed a low-fat diet, along with Questran, a drug used to reduce high levels of fat in the blood. For the anaemia, which had also been brought on by the underactive thyroid, he prescribed regular injections of vitamin B.

A duodenal ulcer and a slow-working thyroid, two unpleasant complaints but, as she and her trainer were aware, not life-threatening in the normal sense, which was more than could be said for the next patient.

A mother had brought in an eleven-year-old boy who looked pale and ill and was suffering from severe stomach pain. He'd been vomiting and was constipated, and when Ben examined him his abdomen was swollen and tender. He'd told the mother he would like his assistant to examine the boy, and when she'd nodded her distraught agreement he said to Tessa, 'See what you think?'

She'd obeyed. Aware that he was watching her keenly, and taking care not to miss anything, she'd finally said in a low voice, 'Appendicitis?'

'Possibly,' he'd said thoughtfully, his face grave, 'but the pain doesn't seem to be entirely localised on the right side. There are other possibilities, such as intestinal obstruction, like a contraction of the ileum that is stopping the rhythm of it, or there could be peritonitis present.

'I'm not sure what is wrong with your son,' he'd told the mother, 'but what I am sure of is that he needs to be transferred to hospital immediately for tests. X-rays will show what is causing the pain and other symptoms. It could be appendicitis, or an obstruction of the intestine. Whatever it is, he needs to be treated as soon as possible.' He'd turned to Tessa. 'Phone for an ambulance, will you, Dr Martin?' and to the mother, 'If you'd like to take your son next door into the nurse's room, she will stay with you both until it arrives.'

When they'd gone he had said with a sigh, 'That one should have been a call-out. The youngster was in no fit state to come to the surgery, but very often that's how it is. Those who're really sick manage to stagger here, and a lot of those who send for us could have made it under their own steam.'

With the elderly, who had come to him with the ills of old age, he'd listened patiently to their sometimes garbled descriptions of their ailments, while at the same time the keen blue eyes behind the glasses were sizing them up.

When one sturdy eighty-year-old had left, looking much more cheerful than when she'd come in, because Ben had been able to reassure her that her heart was sound, and the chest pains she'd been having were probably due to having lowered the handlebars on her bicycle, a fact that had come out in conversation when he'd asked about her lifestyle, he'd leaned back in his chair and eyed her with a half-smile.

'I saw her trundling along the other day, crouched over the handlebars, but it didn't occur to me that it was doing her any harm until today. Sometimes the only prescription that's required is the application of common sense.'

As his hand reached out for the buzzer to summon the next patient, he'd said, 'We get extra funding from the government for our elderly patients. . .and for immunisations, and various other things.'

'So you're out to keep the young healthy so that they live to a ripe old age,' she'd said laughingly, 'and in that way they help to keep the practice profitable twice over.'

'Something like that,' he'd agreed, 'though I've never heard it put quite like that before.'

As she walked back to the surgery after a mediocre lunch of cottage pie and apple crumble, Gaynor Banks, Dr Brown's receptionist, caught up with her and Tessa gave the small middle-aged blonde a friendly smile.

'Hi. How are you?' she said.

The other woman glanced at her quickly. 'Not too bad, thanks,' she said listlessly, and then, as if making the effort, 'How did your first morning go?'

'Quickly,' Tessa told her with a laugh.

'I wish I could say the same for mine,' the other woman said dejectedly. 'Dr Brown doesn't see many patients these days, so I don't have much to occupy myself with, and the time drags.' She looked pale and tense, and as if in explanation of the fact she went on to say, 'And what I *do* have to do I keep getting wrong. My memory isn't what it was.'

'Are you under stress?' Tessa asked, sorry to see her distress.

'Yes, I am,' she said tearfully. 'And I don't know why I'm telling you, a complete stranger, all this, but I don't know where to turn. It's my son. He's behaving most oddly and I think he's a schizophrenic.

'Have you spoken to any of the doctors in the practice about it?' Tessa asked gently, as her mind grappled with the surprising direction that the conversation was taking.

'I can't. I'm too ashamed,' Gaynor whispered, 'and in any case, he's not registered with our doctors. He's with a practice at the other side of the town.'

'What do you mean. . .ashamed?' Tessa asked. 'There's no call to feel like that when someone is physically or mentally ill.'

'He's doing such dreadful things,' Gaynor said wretchedly. 'The other night he went out with no clothes on. Thank God I managed to get him back inside before anyone saw him. Then the other day he jumped out at some children who were passing, and started yelling all sorts of gibberish at them. He won't wash, and sits for hours staring into space, and when he does talk, it's to imaginary people. Sometimes he thinks he's Malcom X and starts making speeches that I can't make head or tail of. He's only just got over one illness, and now this. His father left us, so I've nobody to talk to.'

'How old is he?' Tessa asked.

'Eighteen.'

'And you say that he's been ill recently? What with?' For a doctor's receptionist, Gaynor Banks wasn't very clinical.

'He kept going to sleep at all times of the day. He would even fall asleep standing up.'

'That sounds like narcolepsy,' Tessa said. 'Was he given amphetamines?'

'Yes. Why?' Gaynor asked nervously.

'They're a strong stimulant. Did your son take the full prescription? He didn't have a supply left?'

'Not as far as I know, but I don't know what he gets up to when I'm at work.'

'And the other illness has cleared up?' Tessa questioned.

'Yes, it appears so.'

'Because if he's been overdosing on amphetamines, the symptoms could be like those of a schizophrenic illness. I suggest that you check it out with your son and your own GP. It could be the cause of his behaviour.'

'So it might not be schizophrenia, then?' Gaynor said, hope dawning in her eyes.

'Not maybe in the true sense of the word,' Tessa told her, 'but if he has been getting prescriptions for the amphetamines under false pretences, there will be a degree of drug dependence to deal with. You *must* check it out. Remember, I'm quoting mainly from what I've read. . .not what I've seen, so you need to talk to someone more qualified than myself. Why have you not discussed it with Dr Tarrant? I'm sure he would be the best person to talk to.'

'I don't want anyone at Woodbank to know, especially Anne-Marie.'

'He wouldn't break your confidence, you know,' Tessa persisted.

Gaynor shook her head.

'I couldn't, and yet it was easy enough to tell you.'

She gave a tremulous smile. 'You've got such an open and honest face.'

Tessa checked her watch. The lunch-hour had gone on long enough.

'We'd better get back,' she said easily, 'or I'll be getting the sack, and you'll be having grumpy old Dr Brown after you.'

'His bark is worse than his bite,' her companion said.

'I'm sure it is,' Tessa said with a smile, that faded somewhat as she espied Ben Tarrant coming towards them with the unwelcoming Anne-Marie beside him.

'They make a nice couple, don't they?' Gaynor said as she and Tessa went inside.

'Er—I don't know,' she said awkwardly as she took off her jacket. 'Are they a couple?'

'That's what we'd all like to know,' the little receptionist said. 'It won't be Anne-Marie's fault if they're not.'

As Tessa applied fresh lip-gloss, Gaynor touched her arm diffidently and said, 'Thanks for listening, Dr Martin.'

'I'm Tess to my friends,' Tessa told her with a smile.

The other woman's mouth quivered.

'I'll remember that.'

Tessa had sat in on Ben Tarrant's consultations for a couple of weeks, and during that time she had discovered that he *was* the practice. That he carried it on his straight, uncompromising shoulders, along with the burden of his father's motor neurone disease, and the past pain of a bride who had called off the wedding only hours before it was to take place.

Dr Brown had a wealth of experience, but he was old and out of touch with modern medicine, and easing off towards retirement, while Dr Patel, although hard-working and conscientious, hadn't been qualifed long himself, and so it was 'beautiful Ben', as. Alice Shepherd called him when he wasn't around, who was the mainstay of the Woodbank practice.

'It's a good job he isn't married,' she'd said one morning as she and Tessa were chatting before the others arrived. 'Ben is under a lot of pressure here, as everybody wants to see *him*. Sometimes he just has to delegate, or he would be snowed under. A wife and family, along with his parents' problems, would be just too much.'

Tessa had listened expectantly and, as if sensing her curiosity, Alice had said, 'He was engaged once, some years ago, to Georgina Graves, the daughter of a wealthy banker. Her family lived not far from here in a huge house in one of the villages. She wanted him to give up medicine and join her father's firm. The glamorous Georgina wanted a nine-to-five man but, although he was crazy about her, Ben wouldn't agree. It seemed to have sorted itself out and the wedding was arranged but, the night before, she called it off, wailing that she couldn't cope with the demands of his job. His job!' she snorted. 'It's not a job to some doctors, it's a vocation, and the selfish madam couldn't see it.' As they'd heard the rest of the staff arriving she'd said, 'He paid a high price to keep his career, and sometimes I wonder how much it hurts, for although he doesn't exactly fight off the women, there has never been anyone since.'

Tessa had been thoughtful as she'd gone to join him for the start of surgery. So that was it. Ben Tarrant had put love of his career before love of a woman. How sad that he hadn't been allowed to combine the two. Maybe he would have been able to if he'd picked the right woman.

He looked up from his desk as she went in, and said with a brief smile, 'Good-morning, Tessa. Ready for the fray?'

'Yes,' she told him with an answering smile, 'though this was the only armour I could find.'

He eyed the dress of soft sage-green wool that made her look like brown velvet and her hair a plait of burnished silk, and said, with rare humour, 'It comes in all different guises.'

You bet, she thought. And what's your armour, Benjamin? A cool blue stare. . .and glasses?

'I've got John Dennison, the young fellow who had the epileptic fit in Alfredo's, on my list for this morning,' he said, as she seated herself beside him.

She'd asked about him on her first day at Woodbank, and Ben had told her that he'd seen him the following day and made a hospital appointment for him, when he'd been given an electroencephalogram along with a CT scan and blood-tests. He had suffered another attack since, and was now on anticonvulsant drugs.

'The lad is very apprehensive about the whole thing,' Ben said, 'which doesn't help, as stress can trigger off an attack. I'm seeing him regularly to keep an eye on him.'

Tessa's mind went back to the night in Alfredo's, and she had a sudden yearning to take up where they'd left off. . .socially. Workwise, she saw plenty of Ben and she wasn't complaining, as he was precise and accurate in everything he did, everything he told her. She was fortunate to have him training her, but she was curious to know what lay beyond the doctor garb. . .if anything. That was all it was—curiosity. Of course it was. What else could it be?

His voice was coming over in cool enquiry.

'You're miles away. What is it?' and, being Tessa, she had to say what was on her mind.

'I was thinking it would be nice to take up where we left off in Alfredo's.'

As she watched his eyebrows rise, her face went scarlet. What had possessed her to say that, especially if he was chummy with the aggressive Anne-Marie, who was most unhelpful whenever Tessa had to consult her about anything?

'What brought that to mind?' he asked. 'My mentioning John Dennison?'

'Yes,' she said airily, as if she hadn't made the pushy suggestion.

He came round the desk and stood in front of her, and she had to look up to see his face. Why aren't I tall and willowy like Anne-Marie, she thought, instead of a four-foot pygmy? and then her lack of height was forgotten as she listened to what he was saying.

'I'm going to Alfredo's tonight after I've helped put my father to bed. It's Alfredo's birthday and he's throwing a party for the regulars. Would you like to come, to make up for last time?'

'I'm not a regular.'

He sighed.

'I know you're not, but I am.'

Her eyes brightened. All her friends had drifted away while she'd been in London, and Dominic and his associates were a bit juvenile for her these days. It would be nice to go out for the evening, even though she had cheeked the invitation out of Ben.

'I'd love to go.'

'Fine. I'm not intending driving, as there will be some good wines on offer. So I'll pick you up by taxi and we'll return the same way. All right? And, Tessa, just because I'm almost old enough to be your father, you don't have to dress accordingly.' The eyes behind the glasses were glinting and the mouth, that was usually so set, curving into laughter. 'You can leave the crinoline at home.'

She found herself laughing back as she told him, 'You don't know what you've let yourself in for.'

His face became serious.

'I do, but I'll ponder on that another day.'

As Tessa was leaving after evening surgery Gaynor Banks caught her up in the passage by the back door and, with a quick glance to make sure there was no one around, said, 'You were right, Tess. It was the amphetamines. Carl liked the way they made him feel when he was given them for the narcolepsy, but as it improved, and there was no great quantity to be had from his GP, he found himself another source, and that is what's been making him behave so oddly. It took some doing to get it out of him, but once he'd told me I think he felt better. I made him tell our doctor, and now he's being treated for drug dependency, which is worrying enough, but I can cope with that as long as there's no further schizophrenic-type behaviour.'

She still looked white and tense, but not to the extent that she had during their previous talk, and, as Tessa told her how pleased she was to hear they'd got to the root of the trouble, Gaynor said, 'I'm so grateful for your advice. I can see some light in the darkness now, and it's all due to your help. You put your finger on the problem straight away, which was fantastic.'

Tessa patted her arm and told her, 'I was only too pleased to help, Gaynor. Any time I can help with any of your worries, you've only to ask,' and then, with mock pomposity, 'That's what we doctors are here for, you know.'

At that moment the kitchen door opened and Anne-Marie came strolling out and, as Gaynor gasped in dismay, said, 'What do you think you're doing, Dr Martin? Running a practice within a practice? I'm sure Dr Tarrant would like to know just what a clever-clogs you are.'

Before Tessa could reply, Ben's voice asked from behind, 'Who's a clever-clogs?' She stiffened. Who did the tall brunette think she was? Her position in the practice was only that of senior receptionist. What gave her the right to throw her weight about like this? Immediately a possible answer to the question came into Tessa's mind. Anne-Marie was attractive and very efficient; maybe Ben Tarrant had given her the right. Maybe they were more than chummy.

'Your trainee,' Anne-Marie told him with a sugary smile. 'She hasn't even started treating the patients on her own yet. . .but she's running a clinic for the staff!'

Gaynor had been listening in horror and, as she opened her mouth to protest, Tessa shook her head. The poor woman had enough on her plate without being involved in surgery wrangles and, as far as Tessa was concerned, Anne-Marie was going to have to be taken down a peg.

Ben's face straightened.

'I see. No, on second thoughts, I don't see, but if Tessa is feeling so confident, I think Monday morning would be a good time for her to start doing her own consultations.'

He had an armful of patients' records and, with a smile for his receptionist, he said, 'For filing, please, Anne-Marie.' Stepping back into his office, he reappeared with his case in one hand and a couple of medical journals in the other and, with a brief nod to the silent trio, went on his way, leaving Tessa with the opportunity to say her piece.

'You heard what Dr Tarrant said, didn't you, Anne-Marie? Get on with the filing, and answering the phone, and handing out prescriptions. . .and let the rest of us do *our* jobs, eh? And if I find you discussing Gaynor's affairs with anyone, you'll have cause to regret it.'

Taking the shrinking Gaynor by the arm, she marched her out into the autumn night, aware that for somebody who'd only been at Woodbank for a couple of weeks she'd been throwing her weight about more than a bit.

'That's the first time I've ever seen anybody stand up to Anne-Marie,' the other woman said, as they prepared to go their separate ways.

Tessa gave a wry laugh.

'I'm finding there's a first time for everything,' and it was true. A first time for practising as a GP. A first time for experiencing the camaraderie, or lack of it, in a suburban surgery, and a first time for admitting to herself that she was more that just interested in Ben Tarrant—but that wasn't a first, was it? It was a second. It had happened before, and the hurt of last time would be nothing compared with the misery she would be laying up for herself now if she let if happen again. To all appearances Ben Tarrant was a one-woman man. He must be. It was eight years since he was jilted, and he was still unattached.

CHAPTER THREE

DOMINIC was stretched out on the couch when Tessa
appeared, ready for her first socal event since joining
the Woodbank practice, and he gave a low whistle of
approval. The dark eyes so like her own were watching
her with interest, and she immediately thought that if
Dominic at twenty-three was impressed, would the
same apply to Ben Tarrant at bordering forty? But did
it matter? She dressed to please herself.

'Give us a twirl, Doc,' Dominic said lazily, and she
obliged, a small slender figure in a blue and red print
sarong skirt with a matching red vest, and a silver
organza scarf draped across her shoulders.

His eyes went to her strappy red sandals with four-
inch heels, and he asked, 'Why the stilts?'

Why indeed? Because she didn't want to get a crick
in her neck from looking up at Ben all night, and so
she told him, 'It should be obvious—to give me some
extra height.'

'And so what's it all in aid of?' he wanted to know.
'Where are you going. . .and who with?'

'I'm going to Alfredo's again. . .with Ben
Tarrant. . .again.'

'Ha ha! Gallivanting with the boss.'

'Absolutely,' she said, with another twirl. 'Alfredo is
having a private party and Ben is taking me as his
guest,' and, adroitly changing the subject, 'What have
you got planned for this evening?'

'Coke and chips, *à la* flat. I'm broke,' he said with a
sigh.

Tessa opened her purse. 'I can manage a tenner.'

'Thanks, Tess,' he said with a visible brightening, and unrolled himself off the couch.

She had chatted happily enough with Dominic while waiting for Ben to arrive, but inside, Tessa wasn't feeling so exuberant. While she was showering and getting dressed, the edge had been taken off her anticipation by two things. One of them was the acid encounter with Anne-Marie Davies, which had made herself appear even more cocky in Ben's eyes, and the other was his making the point about the difference in their ages earlier in the day. It had seemed funny at the time, but now she found it depressing. He would be aware of her age from her application details, so perhaps the remark about being old enough to be her father was a warning, or maybe he thought her behaviour so infantile that he *did* feel old enough to be her father, and she knew she didn't want it to be either of those things.

Ben was half an hour early, and in his own car instead of a taxi, and as she went down the drive to meet him Tessa saw that he was still in the clothes he'd worn for work.

He didn't look his usual urbane self, in fact he looked decidedly edgy, but his face cleared when he saw her and he gave her a frayed smile.

'Hello, Tessa. You look very——' He stopped, as if seaching for the right word, and she thought that as long as it wasn't 'young' she didn't mind. 'Smart,' he finished off, and she told herself philosophically that the comment could have been more flattering. . .or less.

'I thought you were going to use a taxi,' she said, after acknowledging the rather stilted compliment with one of her bright beams.

'I was. . .am,' he said. 'The fact is, I've not been home yet. I've been embroiled in the aftermath of an accident that occurred on my way home. The car in front of me veered off the road and crashed into a tree.'

'What happened?' she asked, her smile wiped off.

'I don't know exactly. The couple looked as if they were arguing, and the next thing I knew they'd gone off the road. There was no other vehicle involved, thank goodness.'

'How badly hurt were they?' she asked.

'Bad enough. They've both been taken to hospital. The girl was the worst. Head injuries, broken bones. Her heart stopped just before the paramedics arrived, but between us we managed to get it started again. The man had chest injuries from the steering-wheel, which would surely have seen him off if he hadn't been belted up, and of course they were both in a state of shock. He should survive, but I'm not so sure about the woman.'

'So you've not eaten.'

'No, but I'm not hungry at the moment. No matter how much carnage one sees, it still sickens. I can have a snack at Alfredo's later on.'

'So we're still going?'

'Of course. We can't have you dressing up for nothing. I can either pick you up later when I've been home and changed, and seen to my father, or you can come back with me now, and we'll go to Alfredo's right from my parents' home. Which would you prefer?'

'I'll come with you now, rather than hang about here,' she said immediately, 'that's if your parents won't mind?'

He was opening the car door for her.

'No, of course they won't. They don't get much company these days. A fresh face is alway welcome.'

'Even if it's one like mine?' she said laughingly.

'Even if it's one like yours,' he repeated blandly.

Tessa was surprised to find that Ben Tarrant's parents lived in a sprawling stone farmhouse at the end of a leafy lane a few miles out of the town, and when he saw her expression he said, 'Yes, it's a farm. . .or was. The grazing land has all been sold since Dad became ill, and now all that they own is the land that the house stands on and the field beside it.'

She was looking around as she got out of the car. It was still light enough to take in the peaceful tranquillity of the scene, with distant hills on the horizon, and an emerald tapestry of fields and trees sweeping down from them towards the farm. Water was lapping against stone in the bed of a stream nearby, and there was the scent of wild flowers on the night air.

'It's beautiful out here,' she breathed, 'so quiet and peaceful.'

'You think so?' he said with a questioning smile. 'I'd have thought you were a townie.'

She thought for a moment. 'I am in some ways,' she admitted, 'but I'd love to live in a place like this.'

'I agree with you,' he said quietly. 'It is beautiful, but it's also isolated. In years gone by my mother loved it—we all did—but since Dad became confined to a wheelchair and needs constant attention, she feels rather trapped out here. That's why I sold my own house in one of the villages and moved back home to be with them.'

'How did you feel about having to do that?' she asked.

'How I felt wasn't important. They were the ones

who mattered. It was something that needed to be done and so I put up with it. Motor neurone disease is a dreadful thing.'

'It would have been difficult if you'd been married,' she said softly.

'Yes, it would,' he agreed, his face closing up, 'but as I'm not, the problem doesn't arise.'

The message was clear once again. Ben Tarrant didn't talk about the past.

'My father has the ALS variety of the disease, which is the most common type, although common is hardly the word to describe it, as there are usually only a couple of cases per one hundred thousand people diagnosed each year, so it's hard lines on the poor folk who draw the short straw. It started with weakness in my father's hands and arms, and I was immediately concerned as he'd always been such a strong man. Then he started with muscle cramps and stiffness, and I arranged for him to have the electrical activity in the muscles measured, and a muscle biopsy, along with magnetic resonance imaging, and there it was. . .motor neurone disease.'

His face was bleak, his voice ragged with pain, and she wanted to reach out and touch him, to offer comfort, and, being Tessa, no sooner was it a thought than a deed.

Ben's hand was hanging limply by his side and she took it in hers and gave it a gentle squeeze.

'That's dreadful,' she said. 'It's bad enough giving that sort of news to a patient, but when it's one's own flesh and blood. . .'

He turned his head slowly and, when their glances held, said with a sombre smile, 'Thanks for the sympathy. I'm not usually on the receiving end.'

'Is that you, Ben?' his mother called, as he ushered Tessa into a large cosy kitchen.

'Yes, be with you in a minute,' he called back, and to Tessa, 'My father can't speak, but he understands everything that's going on. His intelligence is unimpaired, so if you want to talk to him, go ahead. He communicates with his eyes or head movements.'

As he led the way into the lounge of the farmhouse, Tessa saw a grizzled elderly man with a head of thick white hair seated in a wheelchair by the window, with a woman who had Ben's fair colouring beside him. When she saw them she got to her feet, and it became apparent that she also had the same height as her son.

'Mum, Dad, this Dr Tessa Martin,' Ben said. 'She's come to join us at Woodbank for twelve months.'

Ben's mother held out her hand.

'Lovely to meet you, my dear,' and with a gentle smile, 'You look very young to be a doctor.'

'Yes, she's a mere infant,' Ben said casually as he went across to his father and eyed him carefully. 'How've you been today, Dad?' he asked.

The man in the wheelchair shook his head and rolled his eyes heavenwards.

'Bad, eh?' Ben asked, swerving to face his mother.

'Not good,' she said evenly. 'But I pushed him to the end of the lane and we sat in the sunshine for a while, and he's had a little broth, but your father's weary now. . .ready for his bed.'

'Yes, he must be,' Ben agreed sombrely, and then on a brisker note, 'Right, let's get cracking, then.'

'What about you?' his mother asked. 'Have you eaten?'

'No, but I'm not hungry at the moment. I had an overdose of gore earlier and I'm not ready for food yet. Tessa and I are going to Alfredo's later, so I'll grab a bite there.'

As Ben began to point the wheelchair towards the door, his mother turned to Tessa and asked, 'Would you like a glass of sherry while we're sorting Dad out?'

She hesitated. Ben's parents would have had a trying day, and she didn't want his mother to feel she had to play hostess to her because Ben had brought her there unexpectedly, but his father was eyeing her with bright grey eyes and nodding his head for her to accept, and so she said obediently, 'Yes, that would be very nice, thank you.'

As Ben began to push his father across the room, Tessa went to the sick man and took his hand.

'Goodnight, Mr Tarrant,' she said softly. 'It's been a pleasure to meet you.'

He moved his head again, this time in acceptance of what she'd said, and Ben said quietly, 'I won't be long.'

'Take as long as you want,' she told him, as a lump came up in her throat. There was a serious illness present in this house, and a huge burden for the stoical Ben and his mother to bear, and yet she sensed a tranquil rapport between the three of them that brought tears to her eyes. Ben Tarrant was a very special man, she told herself, a caring doctor, a caring son, the kind of man who would make a delightful husband. . .if he ever got around to it.

With dreams in her eyes, Tessa sat by a mullioned window overlooking the rolling fields, and imagined small Tarrants with hair of gleaming gold skipping around on the grass while their parents looked on fondly. A board creaked up above and she came back to earth. You're getting carried away, Tessa Martin, she told herself, and with sudden whimsy, and why do they all have to have fair hair? What's wrong with burnished brown, like their mother's?

When Ben came downstairs, Tessa's face warmed at the thought of her wild imaginings, and with the keen, clinical gaze that missed nothing, upon her, he asked, 'What's wrong? You look flushed.'

'It must be the sherry,' she said, skirting around the truth for once. She'd had his eyebrows rising once already today; if she told him what she'd been thinking, they would disappear into his hairline.

He'd changed into casual wear, and in a green silk shirt and immaculate beige trousers he looked more carefree. As she got to her feet, he said, 'Mum says, will you excuse her? She always stays with Dad until he's settled.'

'Of course,' she said gravely. 'I hope I haven't intruded.'

'No. It's as I told you, they both like to see a fresh face. The days are long for them.'

'Your parents are charming,' Tessa told him as they got into the taxi that he'd phoned for. 'I envy you them.'

He turned to face her, aware that her usual buoyancy was absent.

'Yes, you and young Dominic had a raw deal losing both yours in such a short time. I remember your mother very well—she was brave and amusing. Your father was known to me, but not to the same degree, as I'd only just joined the practice when he became really ill.'

'Do you remember *me* from way back?' she asked carefully.

'I didn't at first because you've changed, you're older, obviously, and a lot more confident. Your name was familiar when you applied to come to Woodbank, but I couldn't bring your face to mind. I'd seen you during the episode of the milk bottle and it had jogged my memory, but it wasn't until you came for the interview that it dawned on me that you were the dainty little miss with soulful brown eyes. . .and spots, who always seemed to be at my elbow years ago.'

'I didn't have spots!' she protested.

'Perhaps I'm mixing you up with somebody else,' he said, his lips pursing with amusement, 'although I can't really see that happening as it's not likely that there'd be two like you.'

Tessa found herself sharing his amusement. She could laugh at herself, but spots! How dared he?

They were out on the main thoroughfare that led to the town now, and Ben's mind switched back to the practice as he said, 'What was all that about with Anne-Marie as you were leaving the surgery?'

Tessa didn't intend skirting around the truth this time, and she told him, 'Gaynor Banks had asked for my advice regarding a personal problem that was causing her a lot of grief, and Anne-Marie had overheard us discussing it.'

He frowned.

'A medical problem?'

'Yes, mainly.'

'But you hardly know the woman!' he exclaimed. 'How come?'

'I don't know how it came about,' she told him steadily. 'She stopped me on my first day at Woodbank and poured it all out. The poor woman was desperate to tell somebody and I suppose I just happened to be there. It was a very private thing, and when she brought the matter up again tonight, Anne-Marie started making sarcastic comments.'

There was a thoughtful silence, and then Ben said,

'I'm sorry to hear that Gaynor has problems, and if there's anything I can do to help she has only to ask, but I feel that I must point out that, of the two of them, Anne-Marie is the far bigger asset to the practice. She is hard-working, efficient, knowledgeable——'

'And attractive, with legs a mile long,' she finished for him.

'Yes, that also,' he said, straight-faced, 'but we're talking business, Tessa. Right?'

'I know, but I thought tonight was a social occasion?'

His jaw slackened as he said, 'Yes, it is. I'm sorry. But there is just one more thing that needs to be said before we relax and forget about suffering mankind for a couple of hours.'

'And what's that?' she asked mutinously.

'I will not tolerate any disharmony among the staff at Woodbank. For the practice to run smoothly the staff have to get on with each other. Do you understand?'

Of course she understood, she thought angrily. It was big Miss Perfection he should be saying it to, not herself, but of course, Tessa was the newcomer, so it went without saying that she must be the disruptive element.

'There won't be any disharmony of my making,' she told him flatly. 'I like people, and they usually like me.'

'That's all right, then,' he said.

It isn't, she thought rebelliously. I've just been cautioned like a naughty child.

She was tempted to tell him that she didn't want to go to Alfredo's, that she wanted to go home, but Ben would see that as further pettishness, and she didn't want to appear even more infantile in his eyes, so she sat back in her seat, a small, stiff figure, and let the taxi continue on its way.

Ben had eyed her a couple of times with a puzzled frown, but Tessa kept her head averted, and it wasn't until he led the way to a private room above the wine bar that she began to thaw out. Gregarious creature that she was, the sight of their host, bright-eyed and effusive, surrounded by his guests, with music drifting over, and a buffet of delicious-looking Italian food waiting to be sampled, brought her sparkle back. Tapping her foot to the rhythm, she prepared to enjoy herself, deciding that neither Ben's lecture nor the conniving Anne-Marie was going to dampen her spirits.

'Hello, Benjamin,' the smiling Italian said as they greeted him. 'I see that you have brought the little doctor with you,' and he shook Tessa warmly by the hand.

She smiled, wishing her youth and size were not of so much interest to everyone. Ben's mother had commented on the first, and Alfredo on the second. If it hadn't been for the tall blond man at her side having referred to the disparity between them earlier, she wouldn't give a damn, but it was there, wasn't it? A difference in their height. . .and a difference in their ages.

Alfredo was beckoning an attractive young Italian standing nearby to his side, and when he introduced him as his nephew, Enrico, Tessa thought that here was someone more in her age-group, and he didn't even make her pulses quicken.

It appeared that wasn't the case with the handsome Enrico; his dark eyes, warm and melting, were observing her while his uncle chatted to Ben, and in surprisingly good English he said, 'I 'ave come to help my uncle with the business.'

'Really?' she said. 'Why is that?'

'It ees growing. . .and he ees getting older.'

'Yes, I see. Are you his only relative?'

'There is his wife, my aunt Maria. . .and myself. She is over there,' and he indicated a smiling, buxom woman who was supervising two young waiters.

His eyes went to the tall, fair figure of her companion, still being monopolised by Alfredo.

'Your husband?' he asked warily.

Her glance followed his and Ben looked across at them enquiringly.

'No, my father,' she said, with a wicked little smile.

Enrico's face brightened.

'Ah! So we can dance—have a drink together?'

Tessa lowered her head to hide the laughter in her eyes and said demurely, 'I'm afraid not. Papa insists that I stay at his side.'

'Oh, I see,' he said lamely, and with a dubious look in Ben's direction he walked away.

'What was all that about?' Ben asked, as Alfredo left him to greet another guest.

'Enrico wanted me to wine and dance with him, but he very correctly asked first if you were my husband.'

'And you put him right?'

'Yes, up to a point,' she said, as they took drinks off a tray proffered by a smiling waiter. 'I told him you were my father.'

'*What*?'

She shrugged.

'You put the idea into my head.'

There was a glint in the blue eyes as he told her, 'You're asking for trouble, young woman.'

Tessa groaned.

'Why *does* everyone keep referring to my youth as if I'm just out of Pampers?'

His smile wasn't the brightest thing in the room.

'Perhaps for the same reason my age has just received a mention. There would appear to be a chasm between us.'

'Not as far as I'm concerned,' she told him lightly, knowing that the words had a deeper meaning. 'Almost eight years in medicine has taken the bounce out of me.'

'Not all of it. There's plenty left from where I'm standing,' he said wryly, 'and you're going to need it when I throw you in at the deep end on Monday morning.'

She gave an indifferent shrug.

'I'll worry about that then. At the moment I'm more interested in the delicious savouries that are being brought round.'

Ben looked across to where the young Italian was eyeing them in some perplexity, and said, 'The only thing that young man seems to be interested in is. . . you.'

Tessa was tucking in to the food.

'Maybe,' she said with a grin, 'but he won't come near me now, as I've told him that I have to stay with Papa.'

When Tessa thought about it afterwards, it was as if the time had flown at Alfredo's party. They had danced a little, laughed a lot, eaten and drunk, and, her earlier blues forgotten, she had watched Ben with a detached sort of tenderness.

If the puzzled Enrico had thought that the melting warmth in her brown eyes was a little more than daughterly, she hadn't give him the chance to comment on it, knowing that he had only to mention her to his uncle and her light-hearted fib would be discovered.

When the taxi had pulled up outside Dominic's flat in the early hours of the morning, Ben had asked the driver to wait while he saw her safely to the door.

'Off to bed with you then, daughter,' he had said with a lop-sided smile as they faced each other in the doorway, and, drunk with the pleasure of his company and the sparkling wines, Tessa had stood on tiptoe and kissed his cheek.

'*Arrivederci*, Papa,' she had said softly. 'Thank you for a lovely evening.'

As she had turned to put her key in the lock, Ben had pulled her round to face him again and her eyes widened.

'Tessa,' he had breathed, his gaze on the soft curve of her lips and the rise and fall of her sweet young breasts inside the red vest.

'Yes,' she had whispered. 'What is it?'

'Just this,' he had said, and, bringing his mouth down on to hers, he had blotted out the stars and the dark night sky, and it was as if she'd always been waiting for this moment.

When he had drawn away, she had wanted to cry, 'Don't go!' but the taxi had been waiting, the meter ticking over, and it was too soon. . .too reckless. . .to tell him that she loved him.

Tessa eyed the buzzer on her desk with a mesmerised stare. It had kept her chained there, captive, during what had been two exhausting surgeries, and now it was a quarter-past six in the evening and she still had one more patient to see.

As she reached out to bleep them in, she had an uncomfortable feeling that the rest of the staff were hanging about with their coats on, waiting to go, and she was holding them up.

Still on cloud nine after Alfredo's party, she'd breezed in that morning hoping to see Ben before the day commenced, but it was not to be. The door of the office where she'd been interviewed had been ajar, and as she'd passed she'd seen Ben and the other two partners seated around the table in deep discussion with Andrew Freyne, the practice accountant. As phrases such as 'medical audit', 'financial assessments', and 'cost-benefit analysis' had followed her down the passage, it had been a sure sign that such frivolous things as her telling Ben how much she'd enjoyed being with him the other night, and maybe his telling her in return that it had been a zany and marvellous evening for him too, were not going to be on Monday morning's agenda.

As she'd gone into the small consulting-room that had been allocated to her, Anne-Marie had glided in behind her and put a pile of patients' records on the desk.

'Your morning surgery, Dr Martin,' she'd said sweetly.

Tessa had eyed her levelly. There was no way she was going to let Ben's willowy receptionist get under her skin again.

'Thanks, Anne-Marie,' she had said briefly as she took off her coat. 'I'll buzz when I'm ready to start.'

She had done so, and her first patient had been memorable. A crotchety old man had glowered at her from the doorway, leaning heavily on a stick. Tessa had read all his notes carefully and knew his name, and so she had said with a warm smile, 'Come in and take a seat, Mr Whelan. I'm Dr Martin.'

He'd taken a couple of reluctant steps into the room but made no attempt to sit down.

'Where's Dr Tarrant?' he had growled. 'He's my doctor.'

Not today, he isn't, buttercup, she'd thought. Today you have got little Tessa, who is going to do her damnedest to send you out of here looking happier than when you came in, and that's not going to be easy with all the bonhomie you're throwing around. . .and the news I've got to impart.

'I'm taking some of Dr Tarrant's patients this morning,' she'd told him pleasantly, and had been told crustily, 'Not me, you aren't. You don't look old enough. Are you qualified?'

'Yes, I'm qualified to treat you. . .*and* old enough, Mr Whelan,' she'd told him, keeping her smile firmly fixed, 'so shall we get on with the consultation?'

'You know what's the matter with me, then?'

'I've read through your records. . .yes, and see that you've been having prostate problems.'

'If you mean I'm in a state of either wettin' meself or not bein' able to manage it at all. . .yes, and what are *you* going to do about it?' His hand had gone to the belt holding up his trousers. 'D'yer want to have a look?'

Tessa knew that there was no necessity to examine the man. Among his notes there was a hospital report that had been received the previous day, and that removed any need for further examination. She had known she would have to tell him that he was going to need surgery, a prostatectomy, and they would be sending for him in the immediate future. However, in the meantime he had been out to embarrass her and she had had to sort him out.

'Yes, why not?' she'd said briskly. 'Take your trousers down.'

His face had reddened and his hand had fallen away

from the belt, as he'd mumbled, 'Naw. I'll wait until I see Dr Tarrant.'

'You'll be seeing a doctor other than Dr Tarrant or myself in the very near future,' she'd said carefully, not being too happy about how he was going to take the news. 'We've heard from the hospital regarding the tests that he sent you for, and I'm afraid you're going to need an operation, Mr Whelan.'

To her amazement, his face had lit up.

'That's good!' he'd exclaimed, slapping his thigh. 'Not only will they put my waterworks right, but I'll have a rest and some decent grub for a change. It's no joke looking after yourself at my age.'

'No, I'm sure it isn't,' she'd agreed weakly, with a prayer in her heart that they weren't all going to be like him.

There'd been no self-pity in the way he'd said it, it had been just a statement of fact, from a tough and tetchy old man who'd had his day made by being told he needed surgery.

On his way out he'd turned in the doorway and grunted, 'I'd still rather have seen Dr Tarrant.'

'Yes, well, maybe next time, when you've had your operation, you will get to see him,' she'd said patiently, and he'd hobbled on his way.

Her watch had said she'd been with him a quarter of an hour and it hadn't even included an examination. So much for timing!

It had been a bad start and things hadn't seemed to improve much, although there had been some helpful and agreeable patients, but it was the timing and the eye-to-eye situation that she found the most stressful. In hospital medicine she'd usually been with another student, or a senior doctor, when dealing with either in- or outpatients, and there'd always been somewhere to escape to for a few seconds if one didn't know what to do or what to say, but in a small consulting-room, with the relentless buzzer at her elbow, and the anxious sufferer's face only inches away, it was a different ball game.

Ben had popped his head round the door a couple of times and raised a questioning eyebrow, and each time she'd managed to give him a reassuring smile, but it had felt as if the day would never end.

Thankfully, the last patient was a little boy with a cough, serious enough to the child and his mother, but to Tessa a blessed relief, because when she examined him it proved to be just that, an irritating cough. There was no sore throat, swollen glands, or fluid on his chest. Something, perhaps a very dry atmosphere, had irritated the membranes in his throat, and she prescribed a bottle of soothing linctus.

When they'd gone Tessa swept her prescription-pad and pens into the drawer and grabbed her coat, praying that there wouldn't be a sneering Anne-Marie or an agitated Gaynor waiting to be let off the leash. When she went outside, the reception area was deserted, except for Ben leaning patiently against the counter.

'Where is everyone?' she asked.

'Gone home,' he told her. 'It is half-past six.'

Seeing retaliation as the best form of defence, she said in a voice that wasn't as casual as she'd have liked, 'You wouldn't want me to have rushed through it on my first day, would you?'

The blue eyes behind the glasses were giving nothing away as he replied, 'No, of course not. How's it gone?'

She wanted to boo-hoo, and tell him that it had been nerve-racking, give her hospital life any day, but she could hear herself telling him that it was a piece of cake. What a big-head he must have thought her, and when he said, 'Come on. I'll give you a lift home,' she answered meekly,

'Thank you. I'll see about getting a car of my own in the next few days.'

CHAPTER FOUR

DURING the swift drive to her brother's flat Tessa was too traumatised to enjoy the short time alone with Ben. Her head ached and so did her ego, and when he said drily, 'Am I to take it that you're feeling somewhat frayed?' she nodded mutely.

'It is understandable,' he went on. 'The peculiarities of the human race, combined with ill health, are a formidable force to deal with, but you were warned, you know.'

'Yes, I know I was,' she said ruefully. 'Maybe now I've been broken in it will get better?'

'Don't bank on it,' he told her matter-of-factly. 'Let's just say that some days are better than others. I don't doubt that those of my regulars that you've seen today will be passing judgement on you when next I see them. That's the way they are.'

'Great!' she sighed. 'Like old Joe Whelan who started off by telling me I didn't look old enough, and then tried to embarrass me.'

He glanced at her sharply.

'In what way?'

'Oh, nothing serious. He was just trying to make me flip.' Her smile had surfaced once more. 'He was the one who ended up with a red face.'

'The old blighter!' he said tightly. 'Good for you.'

'It wasn't good for me,' she protested. 'He was my first patient, and after him I was dreading who was going to come next.'

Ben's eyes were on the road, and as Tessa glanced

at the chiselled outline of his face beneath the sun-gold hair she thought that he must think her a moaner. He'd been coping with a big practice list for years, with no one to come home to, no loving arms to enfold him at the door, or hold him close in the night. Instead he had parents who needed him, a sick father who would have to be tended in the night as well as in the day, and on top of that there would be the call-outs from his patients.

Forgetting her own doldrums for the moment, she said impulsively, 'Could I take some of the call-outs for you, to lighten your load?'

'Steady on,' he said with a short laugh. 'You haven't even got a car at the moment, and are you really such a glutton for punishment? If you're daunted by taking surgery, how do you think you would feel in someone's home if you didn't know what to do?'

Her face fell. Ben was right, of course. She was behaving like an idiot.

'In the first instance, any calls you make will be with me,' he said. 'Once you've bought yourself a car and are more settled into the practice, then maybe you can deal with some of them, but until then you're with me.'

'You're with me.' The words had a comforting sound. . .and they were exciting, too, but she was well aware that Ben was talking about work, not pleasure. Yet be it either, she knew that was where she wanted to be. . .with Ben.

Pushing the practice to the back of her mind for a moment, she said softly, 'I had a lovely time at Alfredo's party. I can't remember having enjoyed anything so much in ages.'

Now was the moment for him to say that it had been the same for him, but he didn't. He just gave her a long level stare and said, 'Good.'

Her face clouded. So the world hadn't stood still for
him. The kiss that had filled her with sweet desire must
have been just taking advantage of the moment as far
as he was concerned, and she supposed she was crazy
to have expected anything different. Ben Tarrant was
attractive enough to be able to pick and choose, so was
it likely that he would be drawn to a wet-behind-the-
ears trainee who only came up to his breast-bone?

By the end of that first week Tessa understood why
there were more trainees who didn't take to general
practice than those who did, and she had a dismal
feeling that she was going to end up among the
abstainers.

There was still the claustrophobic feeling when she
was closeted with a patient, cornered by a stranger,
who was hoping, in some instances demanding, that
she would be able to provide the cure they sought.
Then there was the timing. She'd improved on that,
but she was always ready to talk as well as listen, and
the schedule sometimes went haywire. And, of course,
there was the dread that she would be faced with
something she couldn't cope with. All right, she had
Ben on one side and Ranjit Patel on the other, both
there to turn to if she needed help, and there was a
drugs directory and other medical reference books to
hand on her desk, but it didn't stop her from praying
that a situation wouldn't arise that made her look
inadequate.

A lone peak among the valleys was her purchase of
a small black Metro from the father of one of Dominic's
friends; she had declined the offer of the loan of her
brother's car of many colours.

'It's there if you want it, Tess,' he'd said magnani-
mously. 'I've got the firm's car, so I can manage.'

She'd shaken her head ruefully.

'I'm not exactly Miss Confidence Booster among the patients of Woodbank, and if I go round visiting them in that rainbow-hued car of yours that *would* put the lid on it! It's respectability they're after, laddie,' she'd told him in sepulchral tones, 'not a bit of a kid in a jazzed-up Mini.'

There had been no further invitations from Ben. His asking her to Alfredo's party must have been a one off, she'd decided. Maybe that was his custom with new-comers to the practice—a night out to break the ice. Well, it had done that all right! She'd been warmed by the memory of his kiss ever since, but there had been no mention of it on his part. He was his usual remotely pleasant self, a tower of strength if she *did* have to consult him, his advice and help there for the asking, but if Tessa tried to bring their relationship on to a more personal footing the shutters came down. Yet he did have fire in him. It had been there when he'd held her close, when his lips had posessed hers, but it was obvious it had only been a spark, a faulty ignition, she'd told herself glumly, but it had been enough to start a blaze in her.

She began to have an uneasy feeling that she'd been judged and found wanting. She would catch Ben eyeing her with a grave, thoughtful stare that unnerved her, that diminished her natural exuberance more than the never-ending parade of the sick, and she told herself that she was crazy for even thinking there would ever be anything between them. Any fool knew that medical romances were on a sticky wicket from the start. The circumstances of working together, the close contact, and above all the pressures, had shrivelled many a bud that was about to flower, and she had a feeling that the word 'romance' didn't figure in Ben's vocabulary—that rhuematism, rubella, and rigor mortis were the kind of words he thrived on.

As Tessa was driving to the practice on Friday morning a white Fiat drew up alongside her at the lights, and when she glanced across she saw the young Italian, Enrico, behind the wheel. He recognised her at the same second and immediately wound down the window.

'Hello! You not with Papa today?' he asked with a knowing smile.

'Not today,' she told him laughingly, and as the lights changed she zoomed off.

It would appear that junior has been talking to Uncle Alf, she thought, smiling at her reflection in the mirror above the dashboard, and now he must be trying to work out how Ben figured in her life. Well, that was soon answered; apart from his role as trainer. . .he didn't.

An Indian mother with her eight-year-old daughter were the first ones to appear when she pressed her buzzer that morning, and as Tessa observed the pretty dark-eyed child she smiled back listlessly. The mother had a language problem and it was left to the child to explain her own illness which, Tessa deduced after a period of question and answer, consisted of fever, sweating, stiffness of the muscles, and vomiting.

It emerged that, although born locally, the child had recently been on holiday in India, and the symptoms had appeared soon after her return.

'I'm going to put you on a seven-day course of ampicillin,' she told the little girl, 'but if you feel worse during that time, or if at the end of it you're no better, you must come back to see me immediately. Do you understand?'

She nodded and, turning to her mother, who had

been listening blankly, she explained in the woman's
native tongue what Tessa had said. Her mother's eyes
widened in alarm, and Tessa, seeing her reaction, felt
confident that the child had communicated with her
fully enough for her to understand the instructions.

Ben came in before she'd had time to summon the
next patient, and he said, 'I see you got the Indian
child. Normally they would have seen Ranjit, but he's
taking the day off to catch up on paperwork. What was
the problem?'

'It might be malaria,' she told him. 'I've prescribed
ampicillin, and told the mother if she worsens, or it
doesn't work, to bring her back immediately.'

He nodded.

'That sounds OK. Have you seen it before?'

'Yes, as a matter of fact I have,' she told him,
confident on her own ground. 'When I was on paediatrics
at the hospital we had an Indian boy who'd been
treated by his GP, but the bug had got too firm a hold
on him, and he was admitted to the children's section
with an enlarged spleen, tender liver, and a mouth
covered in sores. He'd recently been to a part of India
with no chloroquine resistance and come back with
malaria. We actually treated him with chloroquine, and
then followed it up with other drugs to prevent a
recurrence.'

He was turning to go and she said, 'I saw Alfredo's
nephew, Enrico, this morning. We were both stopped
at the lights.'

He swivelled round.

'Oh? Did he have anything to say?'

'Just a quick enquiry about yourself,' she told him
with a grin. 'I got the impression that he'd been put in
the picture.'

He gave a tired smile.

'You mean to say that he now knows the coast is clear.'

'Something like that,' she said brightly, hiding her deflation at the casual inference that *he* certainly wasn't interested, but because he was never out of her thoughts, and this morning he looked less than his usual capable self, she asked, 'How is your father?'

'Not good,' he replied, his face in shadow. 'He's deteriorating, and the pressure on my mother is horrendous. I do what I can, obviously, but I have my commitment here to think of too.'

Tears pricked her throat. He wasn't moaning, just making a plain statement of fact. She ached to help him and, being Tessa, she had to say so.

'I know I haven't been here five minutes, and I'm still in the early stages of adjusting to general practice, but if there is anything I can do, such as sitting with your father to give your mother a rest, or doing her shopping, or some housework, I'd be only too willing,' she said with grave sincerity.

'You're a nice child, Tessa,' he said with a twisted smile, 'but do you think I want to burden you with my problems? Not really. Anne-Marie does what she can to lighten my load here, and I've decided to bring in a private nurse to take some of the strain off my mother, so thanks just the same, but you've got your own young life to live with your own crowd, with guys like Enrico.'

She was being warned off again and it hurt.

'Don't fob me off on to Enrico,' she said tightly. 'To begin with, I hardly know him, and I'm not into hot-blooded Italians. For all you know, I might just prefer cold-blooded Englishmen, and there are plenty of them about!' and on that pronouncement she slammed her finger on the buzzer to summon the next patient.

Michael Wells was an overweight fifty-five-year-old,

who according to his records hadn't consulted a doctor in years, but something had brought him .to the Woodbank practice now, and Tessa was to discover that it was chest pains.

He was a coarse-looking individual dressed in expensive casual wear with jewellery to match, and before she could introduce herself he held out a large paw and said in a surprisingly gentle voice, 'Hi, Doc. Michael Wells is the name.'

'Yes, Mr Wells. I have your records before me,' she told him, banishing the irritating altercation with Ben from her thoughts. 'What can I do for you?'

His breathing was slightly laboured and he had a high colour, possibly due to being overweight, she thought, as she waited for him to explain the reason for his visit.

'It's like this,' he said without preamble. 'I got married for the second time around a couple of months back, and Jacqui, that's the wife, is into this keep-fit lark. She's been going on to me about it, and over the past week I've started jogging, but last night when I was out I flaked out on the grass with pains in me chest, and had to be brought home. Felt a right fool, I can tell you, especially as Jacqui had a house full of her mates from the aerobics class there when I staggered in. I didn't half have to put up with some stick.'

'How old is your wife?' Tessa asked, as a mental picture of a room full of svelte young women in leotards, watching the overblown Romeo lurching in, came to mind.

'Twenty-eight,' he said, watching to see what she made of that.

There were comments she could have made, but she wasn't there to deliberate on the well-known saga of the older husband trying to keep up with a young wife.

'Tell me about the pains,' she said.

'It felt like something pressing on me chest, then it spread to me back and along me arm.'

'Which arm?'

'The left.'

'I see. Perhaps you'd like to remove your sweater while I examine you.'

As she placed her stethoscope against his barrel chest, his heart-beat was fast and erratic, and the eyes watching her anxiously were asking for reassurance.

'It is possible that you may have angina,' she told him when he'd got dressed, 'but I can't confirm it. I'm going to send you to hospital for tests.'

'What is it?' he asked, white-faced.

'It is a heart disease that can be caused by not enough blood getting to the heart because the coronary arteries have narrowed. Angina pectoris is a common condition in men and can start as early as thirty years of age.'

He swallowed.

'What sort of tests will they be? I'm not used to hospitals.'

Tessa gave him a reassuring smile.

'Nothing to be afraid of. They will do an ECG, that's measuring the electrical activity of your heart, and a cardiac stress test while you're exercising enough to create the same problem that you had last night.'

The man's eyes widened.

'Surely that's dangerous if there's something the matter with me heart?'

'Not when you're being monitored by experts. . .and in the meantime, forget the jogging.'

He nodded miserably.

'Do you smoke?' she asked.

'Yeah.'

'How many?'

He squirmed a bit and then said, 'Forty a day.'

'Well, that won't be doing you any good for starters. And drink?'

'Yeah, I drink. Who doesn't?' he said, getting edgy now.

Lots of folk, she could have told him, but they're in the minority these days.

He tutted angrily.

'It's good, this is! I've slaved all me life, and now I've got it made, I'm going to snuff it.'

'Nothing of the kind,' she told him firmly. 'If it is angina you should be able to lead a reasonably normal life as long as you don't exercise too strenuously. You'll just have to be careful what you get up to.'

'What? That as well?' he said miserably, and as the vision of the nymph in the leotard came back to her mind, Tessa gave him a sympathetic smile.

'It's my silver wedding in a couple of weeks,' Jean Carswell said as they went to lunch together in the café around the corner from the surgery. 'I'd sent out the invitations before you came, and as everyone from the practice is coming, I wondered if you would like to come too, Tessa?'

'I'd love to,' she said. 'When is it?'

'Friday night, a fortnight today. Are you free?'

Tessa laughed.

'Oh, I'm free all right. My social life is not the riot it used to be in London, I'm afraid, but having said that, after a day in the surgery I haven't had a lot of energy to spare for gallivanting, but I'll most certainly find some for your party.'

'That's good,' Jean said with a satisfied smile, and then on a more serious note, 'I hope that nothing will prevent Ben from coming. He's so pressured these days.'

Me, too, Tessa thought silently, but if Anne-Marie was going to be there he would be monopolised by *her*, and she didn't really relish the thought of having to witness that, but she liked Jean, she'd been the first person she saw on her first morning, and it was a pleasure to accept the invitation.

Of the three receptionists, Jean was the one she got on with best. Anne-Marie was too bossy and interfering, Gaynor was a nice little woman, but always so downcast, and so if Tessa wanted a laugh or a chat on the odd occasions when she had a minute to spare, she went to Jean.

On Monday afternoons Ben held an antenatal clinic, with the assistance of a community midwife and the health visitor, and on the following Monday he called Tessa into his consulting-room and said, 'I've got the consultant coming to see my father this afternoon and I want to be there. How do you feel about putting your obstetrics training to good use and standing in for me?'

Her face brightened. Obstetrics and paediatrics—in other words, children—were her thing, and he must think she could do it or, knowing Ben, he wouldn't have asked her.

'You're prepared to let me loose on my own?' she said, with a challenging smile.

'Well, so far you haven't dropped any major clangers. I'll have to take the risk some time,' he said drily, 'and you won't be entirely alone; you'll have the very competent support of a midwife and one of the health visitors. If I get the chance, I'll look in later.'

In spite of his rather dubious vote of confidence in her, Tessa's spirits were lifting by the minute. It had been a long and boring weekend, during which she'd cleaned the flat, done a pile of washing, and shared a take-away with Dominic on the Saturday night.

'No more dates with your doctor friend in the pipe-line then?' he'd asked.

'No, of course not,' she'd told him lightly. 'That was just a welcoming gesture on his part.'

'Certainly beats a handshake,' he'd said with a grin, and she'd thought that she wasn't so sure about that. A handshake didn't leave one with unfulfilled yearnings.

Dominic's own love-life was a sporadic affair, with frequent dates when he was solvent, and a lull when he wasn't, except for the occasions when the girls took *him* out. He was due to sit exams soon for the Institute of Surveyors, Valuers and Auctioneers, and it seemed to Tessa that the only time he got down to his studies was during the periods of insolvency.

'You're not going to pass unless you apply yourself a bit more,' she'd told him a few days previously, but he'd just laughed and told her airily,

'Piece of cake, Tess.'

She'd winced. Those were the words she'd said to Ben, and she'd found to her cost that general practice wasn't that at all, but as she dealt with her morning surgery she was feeling more optimistic. She'd wanted to be involved in the various clinics held at the practice, and now Ben was giving her the chance, and she was going to show him just how efficient she could be. Dr Patel took the asthma clinic on Wednesdays, and Hugo Brown the monthly psychiatric clinic, but it was Ben's antenatal clinic on Mondays, and his childhood surveil-lance clinic every other Thursday that interested her the most.

When Tessa got back from lunch, the other members

of the antenatal team were chatting to the receptionists behind the glass that separated them from the patients in the waiting-room, and she saw that today's recruits were a plump middle-aged midwife, and a tall slender blonde who was obviously the health visitor.

'I'm Annabel Prior,' the fair girl said, and, pointing to her colleague who was deep in conversation with Jean Carswell, 'and that's Beryl James.'

The midwife turned round at the mention of her name and Tessa found herself being weighed up by a pair of cool grey eyes.

'I'm Tessa Martin, trainee GP,' she told her briskly, 'and I'm taking the clinic today, so shall we get cracking?'

'Why not?' the older woman said. 'It's all ready for you, and the sooner we start, the sooner we finish.'

'A truly profound comment,' Tessa told her laughingly, and the midwife gave a dry chuckle.

They were using Ben's room, and Tessa saw that everything was indeed ready. There was a pile of paper sheets for the patients to lie on while being examined, and the equipment she would need was set out beside them: vaginal speculum, dressing forceps, slides, lubricant and cotton wool.

'I'm ready,' she told the chubby midwife as she popped her head round the door. 'Let battle commence.'

Tessa was to see the new patients first, and there were three of them: two young married women, and a third mother-to-be who was much older. The two young ones came in first, and with each of them Tessa went thoroughly into their medical and, if any, obstetric history. Once that was dealt with, the midwife took them to a small room at the side to undress, and when they had put on an examination robe they came back for Tessa to examine them internally. She checked the vagina and pelvic organs for signs that there *was* a pregnancy, and at the same time took a cervical smear and made sure that the pelvis was big enough to allow the baby to come through when the time came.

There were no problems with either of them, but when she came to the older patient, she discovered while questioning her that the woman was taking cortisone for a severe rheumatic disorder.

It transpired that she was a local artist called Zilla Green, a wild-haired, flamboyantly dressed woman with bright restless eyes, and when she saw Tessa's expression she asked, 'What's the matter? Will the cortisone affect my child?'

'Yes,' Tessa told her bluntly. 'You'll have to come off it, otherwise it could cause deformities in the foetus.'

The woman shrank down in the chair and muttered, 'That's terrible! I don't want a child that's not perfect! You'll have to get rid of it.'

Tessa took her hand.

'I didn't say that the baby *was* affected. I said that it could be if you continue to take the drug. Who prescribed it?'

'The old fellow. . . Dr Brown.'

'Yes, well, I'm sure it would have been done in all good faith. I imagine that he wouldn't be expecting you to become pregnant.'

At your age, she'd almost added, as the woman looked to be in her middle forties.

'Why not?' she cried shrilly. 'I'm as entitled to have a child as any other woman!'

'Yes, of course you are,' Tessa told her soothingly, 'and we'll keep a careful watch all through your pregnancy, but you will have to stop taking the cortisone for the baby's sake.'

The woman glared at her.

'And what about me? I'll be walking on two sticks if I come off it.'

'We'll have to find you a replacement,' Tessa said firmly, 'and now if you'll undress I'll examine you to confirm that you are pregnant, and at the same time I'll take a cervical smear.'

'Why?' she protested. 'I haven't got anything catching!'

'No, I'm quite sure that you haven't,' Tessa told her placatingly. 'It's just to make sure that you're healthy down there.'

'And I won't be, will I?' she said hysterically, 'because you people have been giving me bad medicine. It's that Dr Brown's fault! I'll sue him!'

The midwife, Beryl, was hovering, her eyes anxious, and Tessa gave her a reassuring smile. All this was unfortunate, but it was obvious that the woman was eccentric and very excitable, and she'd coped with worse than this. They'd had to deal with pregnant prostitutes from the Kings Cross area when she'd been working in London, and some of those had to be heard to be believed.

The patient was getting to her feet and it was clear there was some stiffness of movement.

'I'm going!' she cried. 'You're not touching me, any of you. I want an abortion!'

'If she carries on like this she'll bring on her own abortion,' the midwife said in a low voice, as Tessa followed the woman to the door.

'Come back when you're feeling calmer, Zilla,' she said gently, 'and do remember that, whatever you think, we are here to help you.'

'Help me!' she cried as she went out, and to the others in the waiting-room, 'They don't know what they're doing in this place!'

The young health visitor was hovering in the doorway.

'Can I help?'

'Yes,' Tessa told her with a frayed smile. 'Give her a cup of tea, and check on her home conditions. She won't let me examine her, so we don't know if she *is* pregnant, but one thing's for sure. . .she's in a very delicate state mentally.'

The rest of the mums-to-be in their various stages of pregnancy were satisfactory, urine and blood samples showed no cause for alarm, and in a couple of cases, where the patients had complained of breathlessness, Tessa had advised that they sleep in a semi-upright position to reduce the pressure on the midriff from the baby in the uterus.

When the clinic was over, Tessa's capable assistant said, 'I'll bet you're glad that is done with.'

She smiled. 'I enjoyed it,' she told her, 'apart from the Zilla Green episode. That was unfortunate, and I intend to ask Dr Tarrant if I can make a house call on her, because if she is pregnant, her age is against her as well as the cortisone treatment, and I wouldn't sleep easy if I didn't follow it up. To have gone into it further while she was in such a state would have only created a rumpus in the surgery, which would have been undignified and upsetting for all concerned.'

When the two of them went to join the others behind Reception, there was a sudden silence and Tessa knew they had been discussing her. Well, let them, she decided. She'd done nothing wrong. It was just sad that the one person who could have had a real problem had been unstable and couldn't cope with it.

She knew that her surmise was correct when, unable to keep quiet any longer, Anne-Marie said, 'Didn't they teach you how to deal with patients at your London hospital?'

Tessa gave her a glacial stare.

'I'm surprised you need to ask,' she said, trying to keep her voice calm. 'If they hadn't done, I might not have been able to persuade Zilla Green to go as quietly as she did.'

'Quietly!' she hooted.

'Well, she wasn't kicking and screaming, was she?' She looked around her. 'Where's Annabel?'

'She's taken her home,' Jean said.

'Good. We need to make sure that she's all right.'

'*You* need to make sure,' Anne-Marie persisted. 'You're the one who upset her.'

'How do *you* know?' the chubby midwife asked. 'You weren't there. I've seen seasoned campaigners who wouldn't have coped as well as this young lass did.'

'Hear, hear!' Jean said softly, and Tessa's heart began to thud. What was it that Ben had said about disharmony in the surgery? It had happened again, and she was in the thick of it.

If he did call back later in the afternoon Tessa didn't see him, and she was thankful for it. Evening surgery was upon her before she could turn round, and when she'd finished, in record time for once, there were only Jean and Gaynor behind the desk.

'Where's Anne-Marie?' she asked.

'Went dashing off,' Jean told her. 'Said she had a date, that somebody was taking her to that trendy wine bar in the town centre.'

Tessa's heart sank even further. That was where Ben went. Was it him that Anne-Marie was seeing? He'd made it clear that he thought highly of her work. Did his appreciation apply to pleasure as well?

When she arrived at the practice the next morning after a miserable night, Ben was opening the mail and, when she looked around her, Tessa realised that they were the only ones present.

He was wearing a beige tweed jacket, a cream shirt and brown trousers, and he looked less drawn than of late. The presence of a nurse in the house could only be beneficial to the three of them, she thought, as she silently applauded the idea.

When he looked up she saw that though he looked less strained he didn't look any happier, and his first words told her why.

'That was some botch-up you made yesterday,' he said coldly. 'What on earth were you thinking of, frightening the poor woman out of her wits. . .*and* allowing Dr Brown to be slandered?'

Tessa stared at him, dumbstruck. So he'd heard about yesterday's fracas already, and as the implication of what he was saying began to register she started to fight back, knowing that if she didn't she would burst into tears, and there was no way she was going to do that!

'As a matter of fact, I thought that I handled it very well,' she told him coolly. 'Zilla Green is obviously a person who is soon upset and inclined to be hysterical, but I had no warning that she would behave in such a manner. However, I've dealt with unstable people before. It was no bed of roses in the antenatal unit of a hospital that dealt with some of London's roughest areas.'

'I'm not interested in your past prowess,' he gritted. 'It's what you do here that concerns me, and so far your efforts haven't been exactly spectacular.'

Anger was wiping out her misery now and she flared back, 'Is that so? Then it will be no surprise when I go back to hospital life at the end of my training! Unless you want to get rid of me on the spot? Anne-Marie must have really bent your ear back last night. I'd have thought you were the kind of person who makes his own judgements instead of listening to tittle-tattle.'

She swivelled and began to walk towards her consulting-room.

'In the meantime, while you're deciding what to do, I'll go and read through my patients' records before they start arriving.'

Ben's face had gone white as he'd listened to her tirade, and now, instead of heaping further criticism on her, he said abruptly, 'I don't make snap decisions, Tessa.'

'Oh, yes, you do!' she cried, her voice hoarse with holding back the tears. 'You've decided I'm no good without giving me the chance.'

'Have you any idea what a disruptive influence you are in my life?' he said with patient weariness, and, as Tessa grappled with the meaning of *that* remark, he walked past her into his room and closed the door, and for the life of her she couldn't follow him.

CHAPTER FIVE

DURING morning surgery Tessa's thoughts kept turning to Zilla Green. She'd intended to ask Ben if she could visit the woman, but in their heated exchange earlier she hadn't got around to it, and if she suggested it now it was going to look like a guilt trip. Yet she couldn't just do nothing. A distraught patient shouldn't be neglected because of wrangles in the practice, and tomorrow she would be occupied as it was her day for training. So it would have to be today, she decided, as the last patient departed.

While she was debating what to do without further argument with Ben, Annabel Prior popped her head around the door, and when she saw the attractive young health visitor Tessa thought that here was someone who could put her in the picture about Zilla.

'Come in,' she beckoned, with a warm smile. 'You're just the person I need to see.'

'About Zilla?' she said immediately.

'Yes. How did you guess?' she said wryly. 'I've been wondering what happened when you took her home.'

'Not a lot,' Annabel said easily. 'We gave her a cup of tea as you suggested, and all the time she was creating about Dr Brown and the cortisone. Then I drove her home and discovered the place was in a bit of a shambles. Paint and canvas everywhere. . .and cats. I don't know how many. I lost count.'

Tessa groaned.

'No signs of a father-to-be, then?'

'Not at that moment. . .no, but there were plenty of

empty wine bottles hanging around, although Zilla could have been responsible for those. Hardly a healthy atmosphere to bring a baby into, is it? But, as we both know, infants can thrive in some strange surroundings.'

'Was she calmer when you left her?' Tessa asked.

'Yes. I think by then she'd got it all out of her system.'

Annabel appeared quite unruffled by the previous day's hiccup and Tessa had to admire her calm. She was serene and competent, and for a miserable moment Tessa wished that she were like that, instead of an impetuous little firecracker.

'I intend to visit her,' she told Annabel, 'or, if that's not possible, maybe Dr Tarrant will call on her. She needs monitoring, and it's imperative that we make sure that she *is* pregnant. I half hope that she isn't, so that there will be no feedback from the cortisone and no problems because of her age. Her records show that she's forty-five, and if it is a first baby, well. . .'

'Have you discussed her with Dr Tarrant?' Annabel asked.

'Yes, after a fashion,' she said wryly. 'He's been told about what happened and thinks I botched it up.'

'Rubbish!' the young health visitor said. 'Somebody should have warned you about Zilla Green—she's weird and unpredictable.'

'Yes, well, I know now,' Tessa said with a sigh, 'and I'm going to have to talk to him about it, but first of all I'm going home for my lunch. I usually eat at the place around the corner, but today I feel the need to get away from here for a couple of hours. I'll be back in time for evening surgery if anybody wants me.'

When she arrived at the flat, Tessa made herself a sandwich and poured a glass of milk, sitting pensively with them in front of her. She needed time to think.

After the row with Ben earlier, surgery had been on her almost immediately, and apart from her brief chat with Annabel there had been no time to sort out the implications of those fraught few minutes.

It was clear that she wasn't going to get very far at the Woodbank practice. She was the perfect example of a square peg in a circular situation, but, she thought rebelliously, unless Ben decided to get rid of her before the twelve months were up, she was going to stick it out. She *was* a good doctor. Obviously general practice wasn't going to be her forte, and once the year was up they wouldn't see her heels for dust, but there was no way she was going to be driven away by narrow-thinking people. She was made of sterner stuff than that. Her fellow trainees in London would vouch for that. If it meant eleven months of misery. . .so be it.

A couple of urgent rings on the doorbell brought her out of her reverie and she found herself sighing again. She'd been hoping for a couple of hours alone, but it looked as if Dominic had decided to come home to lunch too, and had forgotten his key into the bargain.

'Hello, Tessa,' Ben Tarrant said when she opened the door. 'Can I come in?'

She wasn't exactly surprised to see him, although she would have thought he could have waited until she got back to the surgery to tell her that she wasn't satisfactory, but of course, their earlier bust-up had included her giving him a piece of her mind in no uncertain terms, and it figured that he wouldn't want her around much longer. He probably didn't want to have to wait until evening surgery, and, as she showed him into Dominic's small lounge, Tessa was already wondering if another practice would take her on after this. She could just see the report to the Medical Council—

incompetent, rude, overconfident—there was no end to the damning words that came to mind.

'Would you like to sit down?' she said stiffly.

Ben nodded, and lowered his long length into a ramshackle armchair. Neither of them spoke for a moment, and Tessa thought grimly that *she* wasn't going to break the silence. For one thing, her legs had turned to jelly, her heart was slamming frantically against her ribs, and it was because seeing Ben seated there in front of her was making her ask herself if she could cope with a life that didn't include him. But if his reason for being there was what she thought it was, she would have no choice.

'I've come to apologise,' he said quietly, his steady blue gaze upon her. 'The Tessa Martin Fan Club have been ganging up on me. First it was Beryl James, who had supposedly called in to check a patient's records, but she managed to mention while doing so that she'd been very impressed with the way you'd handled Zilla Green, and the way you took the clinic generally. Jean Carswell, who happened to be standing nearby, said that she was of the same opinion, and then I had a visit from a young lady that I hold in high regard. Annabel Prior is one of the best health visitors we've had. A hard-working, tranquil young woman, I would take her word any time, and she had nothing but good to say about you also—that you'd handled Zilla Green very well, and were concerned enough to ask her to take the lady home and check her out.'

Tessa was listening to him open-mouthed. The staff at the surgery had backed her up like that! She felt weepy and humble, but did it alter anything?

'I'm grateful for their support, but it's your opinion that I'm concerned about,' she told him with grave, youthful honesty.

Ben cleared his throat and Tessa saw a pulse flicker in his neck, but his clear gaze didn't falter as he told her, 'My opinion only matters as far as the surgery is concerned. The smooth running of it and the well-being of the patients is of paramount importance to me, and I flew off the handle because I thought it was in jeopardy. I was wrong. I admit it, and I'd like us to start again as colleagues. . .and friends. What do you say?'

What could she say? He was as sincere in this as in everything else he did, and she nodded mutely.

'I'm forgiven then?' he persisted.

'Yes, of course,' she told him, with the generosity that was so much a part of her, but, unable to help herself, she had to say wryly, 'You didn't mention Anne-Marie among my supporters?'

'Er—no,' he agreed, 'but can I assure you that when we talked this morning I hadn't spoken to her since before you took the clinic.'

'You didn't take her to Alfredo's last night?'

The question was out before she could stop it, and he said immediately, his eyes widening, 'No, of course not. I spent the evening with my father, so that my mother could have a rare night out with friends.

'I *don't* listen to tittle-tattle, Tessa,' he said heavily, 'not in the way you meant it. It was Hugo—Dr Brown—who told me what had happened. He'd called back at the surgery during the afternoon for some reason and heard the Zilla Green episode, and I suppose, because he was incensed at being criticised in front of all those in the waiting-room, his version of it could have been somewhat acerbic. He's been a good doctor in his time, none better, but these days I think he's more interested in a hole on the golf course than a hole in the heart.'

He got to his feet and said, 'I must go. I have some calls to make.'

'That reminds me of something I wanted to discuss with you,' Tessa told him.

'What is it?' he asked, eyeing her keenly.

'I'd like to follow up Zilla Green's visit to the surgery yesterday with a house call, but I wasn't sure whether you'd want me to. I thought you might want to visit her yourself.'

She wanted him to suggest that they go together, but he didn't.

'Yes, I do,' he said briskly. 'She is one of the calls I'm about to make. I want to examine the woman for myself. Leave it with me. You've had enough aggro from her for one week.

There might be a truce, she thought dismally, as he moved towards the door, but he wasn't exactly hankering for her company. She would have to console herself that at least the air had been cleared between them, and he'd wasted no time in doing it.

On the doorstep he said, 'I believe you're going to Jean's silver-wedding party?'

'Yes, I am,' she said, her eyes brightening. 'I'm looking forward to it.'

'Maybe you'll save me a dance?' and this time his smile was the kind that lit up the chiselled lines of his face.

Oh, she would save him a dance all right, she thought wistfully. She'd put the rest of her life on hold if he asked her to, just as long as he would be there for her at the end of it. But it wasn't likely, was it? They might be friends again, but Ben kept making it clear that their relationship was purely professional, that she wasn't his type.

'Where is it to be held?' she asked curiously. If there
was to be dancing, it hardly sounded like a house party.

'Have a guess?' he said, with a boyish grin.

'Not Alfredo's?'

'Right first time. It will give you the chance to meet
Alfredo's heir presumptive again.'

Here we go again, she thought. I'm being pointed in
another direction.

'Oh, goody,' she said sweetly. 'I can't wait.'

Ben's gaze faltered for a second and she saw colour
rise on the fair skin of his neck, but he left it at that.

'I'll see you later, then, Tessa,' he said crisply, and
to her amazement he patted her cheek gently, and it
was all she could do to stop herself from grabbing his
hand and holding it there.

'I've seen Zilla Green,' Ben said, when they met briefly
before evening surgery. 'What a shambles! The woman
can obviously paint, as there were some impressive
water-colours spread around the place, but as to getting
down to the basics of civilised living. . .well!'

'*Is* she pregnant?' Tessa asked.

''Fraid so, and, from some of the remarks she made
while I was examining her, I don't think she's too sure
who the father is.'

'What a mess,' she said sadly.

'Life is what we make it, Tessa,' he said gravely,
'although sometimes it seems as if the unkind fates are
bent on giving us a shove in the wrong direction,' and
on that sombre note they separated, each to their
consulting-rooms where the mesmeric buzzers awaited
them.

A gang of trainee GPs decided to go for a meal after
their day on the course run by the Department of

Postgraduate Medicine, and Tessa went with them.
The easy camaraderie and the student atmosphere were
balm to her disillusions about general practice, and as
they ate in a local pizza parlour the talk revolved
around their experiences in the surgeries of various
practices. She wasn't the only one having second
thoughts, Tessa found, though some of their experiences were less depressing than her own.

A quiet, red-haired lad called Mike told them about
the woman who'd stripped completely to have her
finger examined, and how his face had been redder
than his hair, while another had them in stitches as he
described how a small boy he'd been examining had
slipped a pet mouse into his pocket.

'What did you prescribe?' one of them chortled.

'A clip round the ear,' the victim said sourly.

'What about you, Tessa?' one of the girls in the
group said. 'Are you going to opt for general practice?'

'I don't know,' she said slowly. 'I thought the pressures were bad enough during hospital training, but at
least you've got somewhere to hide. . .you can walk
away for a while, but in general practice they've got
you pinned down, and woe betide you if you get it
wrong.'

'Have you had any problems?' they wanted to know.

'Yes, I have,' she admitted with a rueful smile,
'though I'm in remission at the moment, but I don't
doubt that there's another catastrophe around the
corner.'

She wasn't going to tell them that her biggest problem was that she'd fallen in love with the man who was
training her. . .again!

In the period between the truce and Jean's party, Tessa
began to feel calmer. There were still symptoms that

had her baffled, and patients who were difficult, but she was discovering that for every difficult one there were a dozen who were uncomplicated, and now, when she rang the buzzer, it wasn't reluctantly, with her mouth dry and heart thumping.

There'd been the woman who had just lost her husband with cancer of the bladder, and because she'd got a urine infection had thought she'd got it too. When Tessa had examined her and told her it was caused by nothing more serious than a kink in her urethra, her relief had been overwhelming.

Then there'd been the anxious parents who'd brought in their two-month-old baby with noisy breathing. It had commenced shortly after birth, but in the last few days it had been much worse, due to the child having a snuffly nose. It was clear to Tessa that the infant was thriving, and the mother said that in spite of the noisy breathing it was feeding well. She was more inclined to think that the respiratory problem was causing more worry to the parents than the child, but when she examined him there was a harsh, shrill sound when he inhaled, which changed in density when he moved his head, yet the chest shape was normal and the lungs not obstructed.

Although she had an idea what it might be, she decided to ask Ben to join her in the consultation, and when he'd examined the little one he said, 'What's your opinion, Dr Martin?'

'I think it could be a softening of the cartilage of the larynx.'

'Laryngomalacia,' he said with an approving nod, and turning to the worried parents, 'It isn't a serious condition. In fact, it's fairly common. We think that there is some softness around the larynx which collapses when he breathes, and causes the noise that has been concerning you. This kind of thing can persist for up to a year, but as the baby grows older the obstruction will decrease and the airway become clear. Nevertheless, I'm going to recommend that your little one is given a barium swallow. That way we can make sure that our diagnosis is correct.'

When they'd gone, Ben told Tessa smilingly, 'Well done! We'll make a GP of you yet,' and then, suddenly becoming serious again, 'that's if you want to be one.'

It brought to mind the conversation she'd had with her fellow sufferers in the pizza parlour and, with her candid brown gaze meeting his, she told him, 'Some of the students on the course asked me that.'

'And what did you say?'

There was something in his voice that was more than just curiosity—an intensity that made her blood run warm. Did Ben care about what she was going to decide, she wondered? Hardly. It was early days yet. She'd a long way to go before she made her decision, and it wouldn't be as quick as the other one, the all-important one that her heart had made. There'd been no dithering about that. She loved him, and if he asked her to practise medicine on the moon she would do it. . .as long as he was there!

'Well?'

He was waiting for her answer, and with her usual reckless honesty she told him, 'I told them I didn't know. That I was in a period of remission, but no doubt it wouldn't last.'

Ben threw back his head and laughed, and she had to join in.

'You really are the most unusual girl I've ever met. You're like a breath of fresh air blowing through my life, or perhaps I should say a force ten gale, and whatever grief you are going to cause me in the future, and I've no doubts on that score, I suppose it will be worth it just to have known you.'

'Is that how you really see me?' she asked wistfully. 'You don't see me as a competent woman of the world?'

'Oh, I see you as that as well, and a host of other things besides, and one day when I've got the time I'll tell you what they are.'

Her heart was beating faster. What did he mean by that? Whatever it was, he wasn't going to enlighten her. With a fatherly pat on the head, he said, 'I've still got patients waiting, if you haven't, Dr Martin,' and he went back to his own sanctum.

The Carswells' party was in the same room that Alfredo had used for his own a few weeks ago, and when Tessa arrived, having dashed home to shower and change after evening surgery, the place was already full.

As her eyes went round the room she saw Ben with Annabel Prior, and their absorption in each other made her spirits plummet. She'd been looking forward to Jean's silver-wedding celebration, and the main reason was because it would be a chance to socialise with Ben again, but if he was going to be monopolised by the tranquil Annabel, so much for that!

'You're getting neurotic,' she told herself. 'First it was Anne-Marie, and now it's the even more attractive Annabel. You've just got to accept that Ben's not drawn to midgets.'

'Tessa!' Jean's voice called from nearby, and when she turned, the grey-haired receptionist was behind her, resplendent in a dress and jacket in deep blue lace.

There was a burly, bald-headed man by her side and she said with a smile, 'This is my husband, Frank.'

As they shook hands, he said with a chuckle, 'So you're the little firecracker my wife's been telling me about. Been livening them up at Woodbank, have you?'

I can do without this, she thought, being described as the local dissident among all these smart folks, but it was clear that the comments were being made in a spirit of jovial innocence, and so she gave him her engaging smile, and said, 'Yes, I suppose I might have.'

Jean gave her husband a playful push.

'Leave the girl alone, Frank,' she chided. 'She's come to enjoy herself, not to talk about the practice,' and in a whisper for Tessa's ears only, 'You look spectacular.'

'Do I?' she beamed. 'Thanks, and may I say that you look very swish yourself?'

'Well, I had to push the boat out for this occasion, didn't I? It's a very special night for Frank and me. We've had our ups and downs like all married couples, but we've got a good marriage and both appreciate the fact.'

Tessa had dressed in a calf-length cream dress of soft clinging cotton with tiny gold rosebuds all over it. The skirt swung in a graceful arc from her slender hips, the neck was cut low, above a tight-fitting buttoned bodice, and the sleeves were long, fastening at the wrist with gold buttons to match the ones on the bodice, that had been fashioned in the same shape as the pattern on the fabric.

The gold necklace that had belonged to her mother hung round her slender neck, and huge gold hoops swung from her ears below the burnished strands of her hair.

Brown high-buttoned boots in soft clinging leather, with platform soles, embraced the hem of the dress, and as she tapped her feet to the music that a DJ was churning out she was hoping that her role of the evening wasn't going to be that of wallflower.

When she'd looked at herself in the mirror before leaving the flat she'd thought that she looked older, more sophisticated. . .and taller, until she'd compared herself to Ben and his other long-legged admirer.

'So, you've arrived,' he said suddenly from beside her as the Carswells moved away to mix with their guests.

It wasn't like him to state the obvious, and she said with an equal lack of spontaneity, 'Yes, I have,' and, taking in his immaculate grey suit and pristine white shirt, 'It was a bit of a rush, though. How do you come to be here so soon?'

He looked happy and relaxed, for once, and she thought that it must be a relief to be able to shelve his responsibilities for a while.

'Annabel kindly invited me round to her place for a bite, and I changed there. I was called out after surgery to a sick child and she happened to be there on a routine visit, and as I'd taken a change of clothes with me this morning in case of that sort of occurrence, it worked out well.'

'That *was* convenient,' she said politely.

He was eyeing her in a puzzled fashion.

'Yes, it was, but what's the matter, Tessa? You've lost your sparkle.'

'Nothing is the matter with me,' she said flatly. 'If I seem dull, it's because of the company you've just left.'

'What? You're not making sense.'

'Perhaps not, but that's not unusual for me, is it?'

He was looking at her blankly, and then, adding to her deflation he said, as if he thought she needed humouring, 'I see your friend Enrico is here. He's had his eye on you ever since you came in, but he's bogged down at the moment putting the finishing touches to the buffet. I'd like to bet he'll be over the minute he's free.'

'I wasn't aware that you were running a dating agency,' she said stonily, as the hurt of being put to one side again tore at her. 'If I want male company, I'm quite capable of finding it for myself!'

Ben put out his hand in a placatory gesture.

'All right. I get the message. I'm to mind my own business.'

He took her hand in his, and said softly, as if nothing was going to banish his good humour, 'Let's dance, Tessa,' and as the music struck up he drew her towards the small area set aside for that purpose.

She would have given anything to be able to keep up the cold front and refuse, but she hadn't the strength of will to pass up the chance of being held in Ben's arms, and so she said with a confident laugh, 'Why not?'

They danced together for what seemed an eternity of bliss. To be held close by him, to have one of his capable hands holding her small one, and the other pressing against her back, guiding her, moulding her to him, with his lips almost touching her hair, was like glimpsing paradise.

'You look a picture of beautiful, glowing youth tonight,' he said softly, 'It makes me wish. . .' His voice trailed away and she tilted her head back to see his face in the soft lights of the room.

'Wish what?' she prompted gently.

'Nothing,' he told her as the music stopped, and in the same instant Enrico appeared beside them.

Tessa sighed. She didn't know who to be the most annoyed with, the band for ceasing to play at that precise moment, Enrico for singling her out, or Ben, for being so aggravating. If she had to make a choice it would be him. For a delightful moment she'd thought he was about to remove the barricades, and allow her behind his reserve, but no, she should have known better.

Enrico was asking if she would like to dance and Ben murmured, 'Didn't I tell you?' and sauntered off to where Annabel was chatting to the Carswells.

Tessa glared at the young Italian.

'Aren't you supposed to be on duty?' she asked stonily.

He shook his handsome young head.

'No, I tell my uncle that I want to be with the beautiful English doctor, and he say it ees all right.'

'Did he?' she said drily.

Out of the corner of her eye she could see Ben watching them with an I-told-you-so expression on his face, and she thought irritably that if she didn't watch out he'd be giving them his blessing! She'd settle for a bit of good old-fashioned jealousy, instead of his irritating attempts at the mating game, but Enrico was waiting and, ashamed of her churlishness, she said smilingly, 'I'd like a cool drink first, if you don't mind, Enrico.'

'Of course,' he said, his dark eyes warm and inviting. 'What will it be—sherry, wine, beer?'

'Fresh orange, if you don't mind. I'm driving,' she told him, with her glance on Ben again.

By the time he'd fought his way to the bar and reached her side again, Jean and her husband were about to cut the cake, and Tessa was relieved that the moment had passed when she would have had to surrender herself to Enrico's alien arms, after the delight of being held by Ben.

As speeches were made by the happy couple, and a toast drunk to them by their guests, Tessa was conscious of Ben standing a little apart from the rest, tall, straight, his face in shadow, and a glass in his hand. Had he decided that the married state was not for him, she asked herself, and was she going to end up the same as he, alone, because the one she wanted didn't want her?

It was a depressing thought, and it made her smile more brightly at the young Italian, who was encouraged to take her hand and sweep her into a fast jive that the band had just struck up, and as she whizzed to and fro in front of his dark smiling face, Tessa gave herself up to the enjoyment of the rhythm of the dance, the appraisal of her partner, and the tricky matter of staying on her feet on the thick platform soles.

When she saw Ben and Annabel similarly occupied just a few feet away, she nearly did lose her balance. She was seeing another side of him tonight. He really was coming out of his shell, but not as far as she was concerned, unfortunately.

She had a feeling that to Ben she was a prescription-pad on legs, a stethoscope with long brown hair, or maybe just a wet-behind-the-ears trainee. He certainly didn't see her as a desirable woman, or he wouldn't be so wary of any personal contact.

There'd been a chemistry between them while they'd been dancing, or at least she'd thought there was, but it hadn't taken him long to hand her over to Enrico, and if he thought anything was going to develop there he was sadly mistaken, and so was Enrico.

CHAPTER SIX

WHENEVER Tessa thought about that night in the weeks that followed, she recalled leaving the party miserable and confused, and as she'd driven back to the flat in the chilly darkness of early winter she'd found herself going over all that had happened during the evening, with mixed feelings.

The time she'd spent with Enrico had been short, as his uncle had ordered him back to work when it was time for the buffet to be cleared away, but it hadn't bothered her all that much. He was young, attractive, and danced like a dream, yet she felt a thousand years older than he, and thought with grim humour that she'd the NHS to thank for that, even though everyone she met seemed determined to comment on her youth.

Ben had stayed away from her until the guests began to say their goodbyes to Jean and her husband, and then he'd appeared at her side once more, this time with a light raincoat thrown over his suit.

'It's late,' he'd said, stating the obvious again. 'Make sure that the car doors are locked while you're driving. I'm dropping Annabel off, otherwise I'd be travelling in your direction.'

'I'll be all right,' she'd said flatly, wondering why he was suddenly fussing over her after giving her a wide berth for most of the night. 'How do you think I'd go on if I was called out to a patient in the middle of the night?'

Annabel had come out of the cloakroom at that moment and was walking towards them, and he had said quickly, 'I'd expect you to take every precaution for your own safety.'

'So you wouldn't recommend my going out on my bicycle, then?' she'd said with an airy impudence that was meant to conceal her dejection.

Ben had gripped her arm and shaken it none too gently.

'Stop fooling, Tessa!' he'd said angrily. 'Don't you want me to be concerned about you?'

'No! Yes! Oh, I don't know,' she'd said fractiously, and with a quick wave to the approaching Annabel she'd whizzed through the door, with his disapproving gaze boring into her back.

On the Monday morning he'd been his usual self, as if their mixed bag of emotions from Friday night had never existed, and Tessa had decided that if that was how he wanted it then she had no choice but to display an impersonality of her own, however hard it might be to do so, and in a depressing sort of way it was working.

They saw each other every day, apart from Tuesday when she was studying, spoke with each other frequently—about the patients, funding, new drugs—everything under the sun except themselves, and there was a basic sort of harmony between them with which she had to be satisfied.

Winter had brought with it a flu bug and the surgeries were packed with patients suffering from high temperatures, muscular aches, coughs, chest pains, and all the other discomforts of influenza. This, along with the usual parade of ailments, had all four doctors working non-stop, and Tessa found herself going home each night exhausted.

As usual Ben was carrying the biggest load. Hugo's speed of consultation was now a crawl, and the gentle

Ranjit, although conscientious and hard-working, had not Ben's alert mind and expertise.

Tessa was determined to keep up with the others, but after ten days of diagnosing flu for seventy per cent of those she'd seen, she was beginning to feel that if she heard another cough or sniffle she would scream.

'You're looking a bit peaky,' Ben said one morning when he popped his head round the door for a second. 'This darned flu bug getting to you?'

She'd just opened a window to let in some air after her last patient's coughing session, and he said, 'It's bitterly cold out there. What are you trying to do. . . catch pneumonia?'

'No,' she told him with a frayed smile. 'I'm just trying to blow some of the germs away.'

She'd been hard at it since just before half-past eight, and now it was a quarter to twelve, and he was the first member of staff she'd spoken to during that time, apart from Alice Shepherd, the practice nurse, who had dashed in to ask her to come and look at a patient who had just fainted on the point of being given a routine injection.

'I've got a six-footer in my room and he's just passed out,' she panted. 'He only came in for a tetanus injection and the moment he saw the needle he keeled over.'

Tessa had left her patient for a moment and gone to see to the man, who was just coming round, and as he'd surfaced again she and Alice had exchanged amused glances. It was amazing how many people couldn't face the needle, and telling them that it was only a tiny prick rarely had any effect if they really were afraid of it.

He had given a sheepish smile when he realised what

had happened, and said jokingly, 'I've been like this ever since I sat on a pincushion when I was a kid.'

'Yes, well, don't overdo the fresh air,' Ben was saying, 'that's a mighty cold draught you're letting in. I can't have you falling sick. Ranjit's got this flu bug. His wife rang in this morning to say he started during the night with it and is quite ill, so I've added him to my list of calls. Hugo is still fighting fit and so am I, as we've both had the injection, and I presume that you have also, but then, so had Ranjit, and yet he's still caught the bug.'

He was checking the time, and he said, 'I've still one patient to see. I wonder if you could take her for me so that I can get off straight away? I've got quite a few visits, and I want to call in at home to see my father. He's not at all well at the moment.'

Tessa pushed her hair back from her forehead with a weary hand. Her head ached and she felt quite lethargic, which was most unusual for her, but Dominic had got the flu bug and he was not a good patient. She'd been up most of the night with him, supplying hot lemon and hot-water bottles, and had been relieved to see that he was cooler and sleeping peacefully when she'd left. That, on top of her previous exhaustion, seemed to be taking its toll, and though she was only too pleased to help Ben in any way she could, the fact remained that she would be glad to see the day over.

'Yes, of course I'll take your patient,' she said, 'and I do hope you find your father a little better.'

Ben nodded sombrely.

'There's not much chance of that, I'm afraid, but thanks for the thought.'

He was already shrugging into his top coat and picking up his bag, and she said, 'Make sure that you find time for lunch.'

His boyish grin flashed out, and Tessa felt herself colouring as he said teasingly, 'Who's fussing now?'

The grin would be wiped off if she were to tell him that the fusspot was someone who loved and adored him, she thought dejectedly, but she wasn't likely to do that, not in the present climate of their relationship.

The patient that he'd asked her to see was an eight-year-old girl, a chubby little thing who looked pale and unwell.

'We've all had the flu, Doctor,' the mother said, as soon as they walked in, 'and now it looks as if our Amy's got it too and, as it's usually the one that gets it last that gets it worst, I thought I'd better bring her in for some medicine.'

Tessa gave a tired smile. Her head really was thumping now. The moment she was free she would take something for it. . . Talk about physician, heal thyself!

It looked as if the mother was right, she thought, as she examined the child. It was another case of flu. There was fever, muscular pain, nausea, loss of appetite. It was on the cards that if the rest of the family had picked up the bug she was going to do the same.

'Put her to bed when you get home,' she said, 'and give her plenty of warm fluids. I'm giving you a prescription for paracetamol, which should take away the fever and any aches and pains. She should be over the worst in forty-eight hours. I presume that the other members of your family are now recovered?'

'Yes,' the woman replied. 'We're still a bit wonky, but over the worst.'

'Good, and the same should apply to Amy here in a couple of days,' Tessa said as she showed them out.

When they'd gone Tessa slumped down on to her chair and held her aching head. What was the matter with her? She could cope with stress. . .and exhaustion. They were the names of the game in the medical profession.

Alice Shepherd came in as she was dosing herself, and announced prosaically, 'Gaynor's gone home with flu symptoms. That's two, so far. I wonder who'll be next? You don't look so clever yourself. Are you all right?'

'Yes, I'm fine,' Tessa told her. 'Just got a bit of a headache.'

'What about our fainting patient?' Alice said with a grin. 'Strong as an ox, works on a building site. Was he mortified?'

Tessa managed a weak smile. If she didn't get out into the fresh air she was going to collapse.

'I'm going home for a couple of hours, Alice,' she told her. 'If I get my head down for a while the ache should disappear, and I need to check on my brother. I left him in bed with the flu bug this morning.'

'Take care then, love,' the practice nurse said, 'and spare a thought for me taking the asthma clinic on my own this afternoon. It's to be hoped that Dr Patel won't be off long, as our Ben is under enough pressure as it is. It's a good thing he has you to assist him.'

Not any more, if I don't get out of here, Tessa thought, and off she went.

She was thankful to find that Dominic was up and feeling better.

'Tough, eh?' he said with a grin as he looked up from the morning paper.

'That's debatable,' she told him. 'You weren't exactly Superman during the night.'

'Ah, well, don't you doctors always reckon that the sick are at their worst during the night?'

'Not that I know of,' she said with a weary smile, 'but as you're on the way to a quick recovery, I'm going to lay down my weary head for a couple of hours.'

'*You're* not feeling groggy, are you?' he asked, eyeing her white face.

'No, of course not,' she fibbed, thinking that if she said it often enough it would be so, as there was no way she could let Ben down today. . .or tomorrow. . . or the day after.

Evening surgery that night was long and taxing, with Ranjit's patients added to their lists. Hugo Brown had no intention of doing any extra, and so it was all left to Ben and Tessa.

By the time it was over Tessa had only two things on her mind, a long hot soak. . .and the exquisite pleasure of falling into bed after it, but it wasn't to be so. No sooner had she got home and lowered herself into a tub of warm scented water than she had to climb out of it to answer the phone as Dominic was nowhere to be seen, his recovery apparently having escalated.

'Tessa?' Ben's voice said crisply in her ear.

'Yes,' she said, shivering as she stood dripping in the hallway.

'You saw Amy Charlton this morning?'

'Er—did I? Let me think. Oh, yes, I did, the little girl with the flu.'

'It would seem not,' he said grimly. 'I'm at the house now. An emergency call came through just after you'd left. The child is in agony. It's 17, Gregory Street. You'd better get over here. I'll expect you in ten minutes,' and before she could answer he'd rung off.

Her face burned. It hadn't been a request. It was an order, and as she staggered back into the bathroom and began to towel herself dry, there was a sinking feeling inside her that wasn't from any physical cause.

The girl's mother opened the door to Tessa's ring,

her eyes wide and anxious, and when she saw the young doctor on the doorstep she said accusingly, '*You* said that our young Amy had the flu!'

Tessa swallowed. This was awful. She wanted to cry, No! *You* said she had flu, and I was only too happy to go along with you because I was exhausted.

It was the truth. She'd been tired then, but now she was past being tired. She was numb. The address hadn't been familiar, so it had been a case of leafing frantically through the street directory, and then every set of traffic-lights had been against her, and when she'd got out of the car the chill wind in the street had only added to the ice around her heart.

'Dr Tarrant's here,' the woman said shrilly, leading the way to a small bedroom at the back of the terraced house, 'an' he doesn't think it's flu. He's sent for an ambulance!'

Tessa felt herself cringing. This was all she needed. . .a wrong diagnosis! So much for being desperate to help Ben.

He was standing beside the bed when she went in, his face tight and unsmiling, and Tessa thought that she would die if he dressed her down in front of the mother and child, but he merely said coldly, 'We have an inflamed appendix here, Dr Martin. It may even be peritonitis. The discomfort you were told about this morning has accelerated and is now so severe that I am having the child admitted to hospital for a possible appendicectomy. The ambulance is on its way.'

'*She* said it was flu!' the outraged mother cried.

'Yes, well, the symptoms of appendicitis in the early stages can be mistaken for flu,' Ben said evenly. 'And Dr Martin is not yet a fully qualified GP.'

Nor ever likely to be, at this rate, Tessa thought

miserably as he defended her, and there was the old longing inside her to be back on the wards.

'Oh. I see. So she's only learning?'

Was there a note of reprieve in the woman's voice?

'Yes,' Ben told her in the same even tone, 'and we all have to do that at some time or other.'

If he had intended saying anything further, he was prevented by the sound of a cheery voice calling up the stairs, 'Anybody at home?' The ambulance had arrived.

When it had gone, taking the child and her mother to the local infirmary Ben and Tessa were left standing beside their cars on the pavement, and now that they were alone he wasted no time in saying his piece.

'I just can't believe this,' he gritted. 'What were you thinking of? You let the woman diagnose her own child! We're not running a DIY surgery, you know. She told you that Amy had flu, and without any examination or further questioning you accepted what she said. You've put the reputation of the practice at risk by your carelessness. I was beginning to think that I'd actually found a trainee who was first-class GP material, and you let me down like this!'

Tessa's head was banging, there was a strange tingling sensation in her hands, and treacherous tears were not far off. The last thing she would ever want to do was let him down, but he was right. That was exactly what she'd done. The little toughie who'd been so convinced of her youthful invincibility had let tiredness affect her judgement, and she didn't understand it. There'd been times in Theatre and on the wards when she'd been dropping in her tracks, but it had never affected her mental powers.

'Surely you realised there was more to it than flu

when the mother told you about the child's constipation?' he was continuing remorselessly.

Tessa's mouth dropped open.

'That was never mentioned—if it had been I would——'

'Mrs Charlton said that she told you Amy had been very constipated,' he rapped back, and it was at that moment she began to fight back.

'She did not!' she cried. 'Even I, in my innate stupidity, know that constipation is not a symptom of flu, but all the other things she described were, and as she said that all the rest of the family had been ill with it, I——'

'You thought you'd take her word for it,' he said with grim irony.

'Yes, I did,' she flared, 'and I'm sorry. I know I'm at fault, but perhaps when I've been swanning among the patients as long as you have, I'll be just as clever. Until then, I'm afraid I will have to remain mediocre.'

Her voice softened and there was pleading in it as she said, 'It's just that I'm so tired, Ben. I can't think straight. I was up most of the night with Dominic, and the surgeries have been so long, and. . .' Her voice trailed away and she bent her head and wept.

There was silence for a moment, and then he took her arm and opened the door of his car.

'Get inside, Tessa,' he said quietly, and when she made no move he pushed her gently into the passenger seat.

'What's wrong? Are you ill?' he asked, when he was seated beside her. 'It's not like you to be so defeatist.'

'I know it isn't,' she sobbed, 'but I'm so tired. I feel as if all my vitality is draining away.'

'Maybe you're starting with this flu bug.'

'No, I don't think so,' she gulped. 'I don't know

what's wrong with me.' Unless it's the effects of unrequited love, she thought wretchedly.

Ben put his arm round her shoulders and cradled her to him, and then, taking a large white handkerchief out of his pocket, he gently wiped her blotchy face.

'What have you been up to that's different?' he asked. 'Have you changed your lifestyle in any way?'

'Well, of course I have!' she exclaimed with a watery smile. 'I've entered the world of the busy GP and my feet haven't touched the ground since!'

'I don't mean that,' he said, shaking his head. 'You've been coping fine. It could be something else. Are you eating properly?'

'Yes, and no,' she told him, pulling a wry face. 'Dominic decided he was going to be a Vegan, and to make life easier I said I'd join him.'

'So you're not eating meat, fish, or dairy products?'

'Well, no, but I'm eating lots of fruit, vegetables, nuts, and other nutritious things.'

'Maybe,' he said thoughtfully, 'but in a few cases a Vegan diet can cause vitamin B deficiency. It's possible that you're becoming anaemic, and that, along with the pressures of the practice, is causing the tiredness.'

'My hands keep tingling,' she told him. 'I suppose that could be a sign of anaemia.'

'Yes, it is. We'll take some blood-tests tomorrow and I've a feeling that I won't be far wrong. Your body is having to adjust to a new eating pattern and it's taking its toll, but we'll see what the tests say, eh? And in the meantime I think we should get you home to bed.'

He was smiling now and her heart went weak with relief.

'A tired GP is no good to anybody,' he said, 'least of

all the patients, and if you're too tired to diagnose yourself, what chance have they got?'

'I'm sorry about little Amy,' she said, burying her nose in the handkerchief as the tears came flooding back, 'but I'm even more sorry that I've let you down, Ben. I did so want to help you, and I'm proving to be nothing but a hindrance.'

'True,' he said with a chuckle, 'but there are hindrances and hindrances, and your entertainment value makes up for the hindering. Tonight's episode was unfortunate, and I have to admit that anything that reflects badly on the practice makes me see red, but you know, Tessa, I get tired too, and I shouldn't take it out on you.'

She knew that any second he was going to remove his arm, the comfort of his nearness would be gone, and she couldn't bear the thought of it. Looking up into his eyes, she asked recklessly, 'Why do you keep me at arm's length all the time, Ben? You're happy in Annabel's company, and with Anne-Marie, but not with me. What's wrong with me, apart from the fact that I'm not a long-legged lovely?'

Laughter rumbled in his throat and he ruffled her hair gently as he told her, 'There is nothing wrong with you, Dr Martin, although I do have to admit there is a problem.'

'And what's that?' she breathed, her lips only inches away from his.

'That there's too much that's right about you, and I'm having to adjust.'

'I think that is supposed to be a compliment,' she said, as her natural bounce began to surface again, 'but I wouldn't bet on it.'

'Good thinking,' he said with a grin and, planting a tantalising butterfly kiss on her parted lips, he ordered,

'Out you get, my unpredictable assistant, and drive carefully. I want you to arrive home in one piece.'

When they got back to the flat, after Ben had followed her home, he said, 'I suggest a good hot bath, followed by a mug of malted milk or something, and then bed.'

'When you rang earlier I was in the bath, all set for an early night,' she said softly.

'Yes, well, you wouldn't have wanted me to keep you in the dark about young Amy Charlton, would you?' he asked gravely.

'No, I wouldn't,' she told him quickly, 'and I shall be praying that my negligence hasn't harmed her.'

He touched her gently under the chin.

'You're only human like the rest of us, my sweet Tess. The snag is that we're not supposed to be, and sometimes it's easier to go along with that.'

By the time the results of the blood-tests had come through, showing that Tessa was indeed suffering from some degree of anaemia, the flu epidemic had begun to ease off, she had given up the Vegan diet, Christmas was beckoning like a bright lantern in the gloom of winter. . .and, the most important event of all, Amy Charlton's appendicectomy had been performed successfully without any perforation of the appendix having occurred.

Tessa and Ben went to see her on her discharge from hospital and found her making good progress.

'I'm so sorry about what happened,' Tessa told her mother. 'The only reasons I can give for not realising what was wrong with Amy are that when I saw her in the morning she wasn't in any great pain, and that I wasn't well myself at the time.'

'That's a laugh! A doctor not knowing herself to be

poorly,' Mrs Charlton said in a friendlier voice than she'd used at their last meeting.

'We're too busy to sort out our own ailments,' Ben told her with a smile, and to Tessa's relief they parted on the best of terms.

'How are you feeling today?' Ben asked as they travelled back to the practice.

'Mentally. . .fine,' she said lightly. 'Physically. . .still a bit jaded, but nowhere near as limp as I was. Megablastic anaemia was the last thing I'd have thought of. Some doctor, aren't I? But now that I'm on this short course of injections of vitamin B_2 and have returned to my normal diet, I expect to be fit for the London Marathon in the very near future.'

He smiled his quizzical smile.

'You being fit enough for the daily marathon at the practice will do me,' he said. 'I should have realised that you weren't well, but I didn't know you'd changed to a Vegan diet, for one thing, though lots of folks are vegetarians and stay perfectly healthy. You must be one of the rare cases where it isn't advisable.'

'It's as you told Mrs Charlton—health care, like charity, should begin at home,' she said levelly, 'but we don't always see what's under our noses.'

There was silence when she'd finished speaking and, as Ben met her bright, challenging gaze, Tessa wondered if he realised that the words had another implication.

It was possible that he did, as he replied sombrely, 'That's true. *I* admit to having been blinkered in the past.'

'And the present?' she persisted softly.

'Leave it, Tess,' he said abruptly, and, with his usual skill at changing the subject, 'We've still a lot of calls to make.'

* * *

'The partners always take the staff out for a meal at Christmas,' Alice, the practice nurse, said one morning as she and Tessa were waiting for the women booked in for smear tests to arrive. 'This year they're taking us to the Highwayman on the Friday before Christmas.'

'Where's that?' Tessa asked, her eyes brightening.

'It's a posh restaurant out in the country,' the nurse explained. 'They have dinner-dances there.' She giggled. 'You should see old Hugo tripping the light fantastic. He's a whizz at the military two-step.'

As they exploded into shared laughter the elderly GP under discussion came stomping past and wanted to know what was so amusing, and when Alice told him they were discussing the Christmas meal he grumbled, 'There'll be a lot more patients to see and prescriptions to be made out before then,' and as the first of the cervical smear recipients appeared in the waiting-room he said, 'And a lot more of them to see as well.'

When he'd gone they exchanged smiles and Tessa said, 'And what was that? The gospel according to Sergeant-major Brown?' and, as Anne Marie bore down on them with a sheaf of the aforementioned prescriptions in her hand, 'And here is Corporal A. M. Davies to read the first lesson.'

'What's the joke?' the senior receptionist asked icily.

'We're just putting caps on heads to see if they fit,' Tessa told her.

'Really! Pity you've nothing better to do,' she retorted. 'I'll bet Dr Tarrant wishes *he* had the time for fooling around.'

'We're not fooling around,' Tessa told her mildly. 'I've just finished morning surgery, and now we're going to do the smear tests, and after that I want Dr

Tarrant's advice about one of the patients I've just seen.'

'So you don't know everything, after all,' Anne-Marie said sweetly.

'I don't ever remember saying that I did,' Tessa replied. 'One only needs to come into general practice to realise just how little one really does know.'

When she went into Ben's room before lunch, he looked up from the papers on his desk and said with a smile, 'You're confused about something, I believe.'

She sighed. Why couldn't Anne-Marie mind her own business?

'I presume you've been speaking with the eyes and ears of the practice,' she said tartly, her earlier good humour diminishing.

Ben tutted amiably.

'She's a darned good receptionist, Tess.'

'She's also an interfering busybody,' she snapped, aware that her pettishness was due to jealousy as much as anything. 'I may be confused most of the time,' she said sardonically, 'but on this occasion I merely needed your opinion.'

He pushed his chair back, tilting it precariously, and, with his bright blue gaze fixed intently on her, said in the same pleasant tone, 'Fire away, then.'

'I saw a man called Michael Wells in the first week I was seeing patients on my own. In his middle fifties, he was showing signs of angina.' She averted her eyes. 'Apparently he has a much younger wife who sounds very fit, and he had been stretching himself to keep up with her. He struck me as being the hard-drinking, smoking, womanising type, and wasn't in the very best of condition.

'I sent him for tests and it seems that he *has* got angina. He's been in this morning in a state, having been told to give up smoking and lose weight, among other things, and he thinks he's going to drop dead any second.

'The hospital have put him on glyceryl trinitate to increase the blood-flow through the heart muscle, et cetera, and obviously he's going to have to slow down but, petrified though he may be, he's making a big thing about not wanting to lose his macho-man image.

'I tried to reassure him, but he was too worked up to hear a word I said, and consequently I wondered if you thought we should bring them both in for counselling. If his wife really cares about him then she is the best person to reassure him, whereas if she isn't made aware of the depth of his anxiety, then. . .'

'What's the age difference?' Ben asked quietly.

'Quite a bit,' she told him casually. 'He was in the construction business, and he strikes me as the type of man who has worked hard, made a lot of money, and now wants to play hard, only to find that he's got to alter his lifestyle somewhat.'

Ben was gazing through the window, deep in thought, and as she watched him Tessa longed to touch the capable hand that lay loosely on the desk. She wanted to tell him that it wouldn't be like that for *them*. For one thing, the age difference would be a lot less, and for another she wasn't a keep-fit bimbo, or he a bar-top Romeo.

As if he guessed her thoughts, he turned slowly and said in a low voice, 'Yes. They will need counselling. No older man or woman should attempt to hitch a ride on the shoulders of the young.'

'Rubbish!' she declared, aware that her voice was high, her heart thumping. 'Although I'm a similar age to Enrico, when I'm with him I feel a thousand years older. It's what a person is inside that counts, Ben, not how old they are,' and, as her customary reckless honesty surfaced, '*I* don't feel as if there is any age difference between *us*, so sleep on that, Dr Tarrant!' and, resisting an overwhelming urge to grab him and prove it, she waltzed out of the room.

CHAPTER SEVEN

IT WAS a grey December morning, and when Tessa arrived at the practice her mood matched the day. The crowded waiting-room, and a baleful stare from Anne-Marie behind Reception, did nothing to lighten it, but as she prepared for the fray she admitted to herself that it wasn't really the weather, or the patients, or even Anne-Marie, that were responsible for her mood. It was the inaccessibility of Ben Tarrant that was causing her gloom.

Of course, that didn't apply to work. He was for ever accessible there, but for anything more personal he was not available.

His father's condition was worsening and Tessa understood the commitment and anxiety that were involved with that, but there were times when he was briefly free in the evenings, or at weekends, when he might have suggested they spend more time together, but obviously it hadn't occurred to him or, if it had, the idea hadn't appealed.

After her laying it on the line that the age difference between them made no odds to her, and doing everything but spell it out that she was deeply attracted to him, she had decided that the next move, if any, had to come from Ben.

He was always ready to talk to Annabel, and to heap praise on Anne-Marie, but she still felt as if she'd been labelled 'trespasser'.

It was just three weeks to Christmas and Tessa was looking forward to the festive season with mixed feelings. Dominic's calendar was fully booked. She was going to see little of him over Christmas, and she supposed that her own life could be as full as his if she could get her mind off Ben for long enough to get to know other men.

As she was on the point of letting Reception know that she was ready for the first patient, that situation was about to change. The door of her consulting-room opened and Ben was framed there, with a broad-shouldered, copper-haired man beside him, and after wishing her a pleasant good-morning he said, 'I'd like you to meet a very good friend of mine, Tessa. This is Miles Callender, the consultant who's treating my father. He's a guy in a class of his own, the best,' and to the man at his side, 'Meet Tessa Martin, our trainee GP.'

When they shook hands, Tessa was aware that here was a man who was very attractive. . .and knew it. He held her hand just a fraction longer than was necessary, and the amber warmth of the eyes that met hers had the age-old message in them.

'It's your staff who're in a class of their own,' he said, with a smile that gave a glimpse of gleaming white teeth beneath a burnished moustache, 'and it looks as if you've left the classiest until the last.'

Tessa eyed him coolly.

Spare me the flannel, she thought.

'I'll bet you say that to all the girls, Mr Callender,' she said sweetly, and was aware that Ben wasn't exactly approving of her flippancy. That was just too bad, though, wasn't it? What did he expect her to do when faced with a smoothie like his friend Miles at half-past eight in the morning? Kiss his feet?

'No, only to pretty little brunettes,' he replied

unabashed, and Tessa had a wild desire to put on a show of girlish ecstasy by pirouetting around the room.

Ben was watching her, straight-faced, and she knew even more that she wasn't pleasing him.

'Miles is on his way to see Dad,' he said levelly, 'before his own busy day starts.'

'Yes, I'm based at the infirmary and the Arrowfield private hospital,' the young consultant said easily. 'I've just been saying to Ben that if ever he wants to bring the staff for a conducted tour around either place, I'll be only too pleased to act as a guide.'

'It would be a matter of finding the time, I'm afraid, Miles,' Ben told him. 'Our days are pretty full here. Take today, for instance—once morning surgery is over we have toddlers coming in for immunisation, and this afternoon Hugo, Ranjit and I have a resources meeting. Then there are the various clinics we hold in the afternoons. . . I could go on forever, but who knows, one day, maybe, eh, Tessa?'

'Yes, of course,' she said with a laugh. 'We could always do a night shift.'

She was behaving abominably, she knew it, but it was so peeving to be getting the glad eye from a man she'd only just met, when the one who filled her every waking thought saw her only as a colleague, and an average one at that. Maybe she ought to respond to Miles Callender's obvious charm. It would be nice to be seen with a handsome, successful man for a change, instead of being a spectator on the edge of the life of an overworked GP. That was, of course, providing the signals she was getting weren't just a leg-pull.

They weren't. The phone rang that same evening and it was Miles.

'Miles Callender here, Tessa,' he said softly. 'I was wondering if I could take you out to dinner?'

Gee whizz! she thought. Ben's pushy friend didn't let the grass grow under his feet, but she had to admit that the fact that somebody found her desirable was balm to her ego. However, being Tessa, she had to say her piece.

'I wouldn't have thought that trainee GPs were in your league, Mr Callender.'

'Miles,' he said, in the same seductive tone, 'and a pretty woman is a pretty woman in anybody's language. So how about it?'

'Yes, why not?' she said on a mad impulse. Why not allow herself to be wined and dined by an attractive man? Just as long as that was all he wanted!

Perversely she dressed with great care in a beige hobble skirt and a peach silk blouse, brushed her long mane until it sprang into shining curls, and enhanced the fine bone-structure of her youthful face with the expensive make-up that she used only for special occasions, and when she surveyed the finished article her mouth twisted wryly. It should be Ben that she was making herself beautiful for, not a man that she'd only just met.

The car was like the man, sleek and flamboyant, and the restaurant a select establishment out on the coach road that led to the hills that she'd seen on the horizon from Ben's parents' farm.

'How do you get on with Ben?' he asked, after telling her that she was very beautiful, and receiving a doubtful laugh for his pains.

'I get on with him very well,' she said carefully.

This man was his friend and she didn't want him to find out that she loved Ben Tarrant. If ever Ben did find out that she loved him it would be at first hand, not second, and the chances of that situation arising weren't looking too good.

'Ben could have gone places in the medical world,' Miles said. 'We were at college together and he was one of the brightest of the bunch, but of all things he chose general practice. He could have made a lot more money specialising like me.'

'Perhaps wealth isn't all that important to him,' said Tessa, the idealist. 'He's an excellent GP. Ben is held in high esteem by his partners and patients alike. He puts all his energies into the job.'

'*All* of them?' Miles Callender questioned meaningfully, the calculating amber eyes looking her over with undisguised approval.

'Yes, all of them,' she told him flatly.

'That's because of the gorgeous Georgina,' he told her. 'She was a corker, but more my type than his. She had an eye to the main chance, and becoming the wife of a junior partner in a local practice didn't match up to her expectations. However, she reckoned without Ben's dedication to his career, and it peeved her no end that he wouldn't give it up for her.'

'Good for him,' Tessa said staunchly. 'Maybe Ben lost out in one way by his marriage being cancelled, but he surely must have gained in another.'

'In what way?'

'Escaping from the clutches of a selfish woman. I'd say he had a lucky escape.'

'Yes, but did he see it that way?' Miles Callender said as he swirled the wine around his glass. 'And in any case, all that could soon be past tense. She's back in circulation, and might be ready to take up where she left off.'

Her mouth went dry,

'What do you mean?' she breathed.

Panic had her in its grip. The spectres of Annabel and Anne-Marie were as nothing compared to this!

'He's bringing her here tonight,' her companion said calmly. 'And I thought I'd like to be around for the great reconciliation scene.'

Tessa's mouth was drawn back in horror, her face bleached with dismay, as the implications of what he'd just said hit her. The first disastrous thought to cope with was that the woman whom Ben had once been deeply in love with was back in his life. That alone was terrible news, but on its heels was the realisation that she was going to be forced to watch them together as a reluctant bystander, and thirdly—and anger was ripping through her at the thought of it—this so-called friend of Ben's had made her a party to his nasty curiosity. He hadn't fancied her at all. The invitation had just been a means to an end.

With eyes cold as ice, she bent to pick up her bag and he said quickly, 'What's wrong?'

'I'm going, Miles, that's what!' she hissed. 'I have the deepest respect for Ben Tarrant and I don't want him to find me prying into his affairs,' and she got to her feet.

He took her hand and pushed her back down into the seat.

'No problem,' he said easily. 'Ben will think it's a coincidence us being here. He'll have forgotten he mentioned it to me this morning.'

Tessa glared at him.

'If you think that, you're crazy! Ben doesn't forget anything.' Including his long-lost Georgina by the sound of it, she thought dismally.

Her eyes widened and the bright colour washed up in her face. The head waiter had gone to greet a tall fair man accompanied by an exquisitely dressed red-headed woman who was almost as tall, and, knowing that she would have to walk past them to get out of the room, Tessa cringed in her seat.

They had been taken to a table at the other side of the room and so far Ben had eyes only for his companion. He hadn't seen Tessa and the outrageous Miles, and in the moment's respite she couldn't decide what to do. If she got up and walked out she would attract attention and almost certainly be noticed by Ben, and if she stayed put there would be a couple of hours' agony ahead of her.

The decision was to be taken out of her hands. Ben had seen them, and he got to his feet and came across to their table. He gave Miles a brief nod and, eyeing Tessa unsmilingly, commented, 'I certainly wasn't expecting to see *you* here tonight, Tessa.'

It was all she could do not to fling her arms round his neck and beg him to believe that Miles's act of complete insensitivity didn't include herself. . .and she could just imagine what the cool green eyes surveying them from across the room would make of that!

'You know Georgina, don't you, Miles?' Ben said quietly. 'Maybe you'd like to come across and renew the acquaintance,' and to Tessa, 'Let me introduce you to someone I knew a long time ago.'

As she got reluctantly to her feet Tessa was wishing herself a million miles away. It was despicable of Miles Callender to bring her here when he knew that Ben had planned to bring his lost love to the same place. Given the chance, she would tell him what she thought about his behaviour and his motives, but for the present there was the embarrassing introduction to face, to a woman that she already disliked when she hadn't even met her.

The prodigal Georgina lifted a smooth, tight face for the kiss that Miles was only too eager to bestow, and said lightly, 'Nice to meet you again, Miles.' Then she turned to Tessa, standing tight-lipped and furious beside him. 'And who is this, Ben?'

'Dr Tessa Martin, a fellow GP,' he said guardedly, as if feeling his way through a field of nettles.

Tessa gave him a brief smile of gratitude. He could have told his ex-fiancée that she was just a trainee, or the practice pain in the neck, or a bit of a kid who was out of her depth with a wolf like Callender, but he'd said none of those things, and she wondered why, because he must be furious at finding her on the scene when he was about to turn back the clock in the company of the woman who had spoiled his appetite for marriage.

She saw that Georgina was quite a bit older than herself, though still very attractive, but during the introduction it was her expression that registered the most with Tessa. She looked miserable and unhappy, and Tessa thought glumly that, if Ben still loved her, the 'little girl lost' approach would be just the thing to ensnare him again.

'I'm sure that you must both have a lot to talk about,' she said politely after they had been introduced and, with a steely glare for Miles Callender, she excused herself and made her way back to their table, leaving him with no option but to follow.

'How dare you involve me in this charade?' she said furiously once they were seated again. 'I thought you were supposed to be Ben's friend.'

'I am,' he said with sudden seriousness. 'It seemed funny at the time. Turning up to see how he reacts to Madame Georgina. . .'

'And dragging one of his staff along for good measure,' she finished off for him acidly.

He was perking up again. 'That was for pleasure, Tessa, pure pleasure.'

'Short-lived, I'm afraid,' she told him coldly as she got to her feet again. 'I want to go home. If you don't want to take me, I'll get a taxi.'

'Of course I'll take you,' he said with a sigh. 'I don't want to play gooseberry to Ben and Georgina.'

'Goodnight, Miles,' she said, the moment he stopped the car outside Dominic's flat. 'I won't say thanks for a lovely evening.' With head held high, and a lump in her throat which felt the size of a football, she went inside.

The attractive middle-aged blonde at the other side of the desk was seething with frustration as she told Tessa, 'I waited ages for a tonsillectomy on the NHS, and by the time it was done my throat was badly infected. When I'd had the surgery, instead of giving me foods that were easy to swallow, they insisted on me eating roughage—crusty, hard foods which the hospital said would help to break away the infected areas from the lining of my throat, but it didn't seem to work, and now, six weeks after the surgery, I've still got a horrendously sore throat that looks like the surface of the moon, only it's got more craters.'

Tessa had been listening carefully. Here was no neurotic whinger. She came over as a strong, intelligent woman who was at the end of her tether.

'Let me take a look,' she said when the woman had finished speaking, and when Tessa had completed her examination she had to admit that the patient wasn't exaggerating. Her throat was a mess.

'I haven't seen you before, have I, Mrs Durant?' she asked as she seated herself behind the desk again.

'No. I've been under the hospital with this lot, but

I've come to the surgery pretty frequently before the operation as I suffered from frequent bouts of tonsillitis. You're new, aren't you?'

'Yes, I am. I'm a trainee,' she told her evenly.

'That's fine by me,' Angela Durant said briskly. 'It's good to talk to a woman, and I've already been to the top, so maybe I should start at the bottom again. I used to be in private medicine, but we've had a lot of money problems over the last couple of years and we had to opt out, unfortunately. Since the operation, the hospital have had me on antibiotics, but they haven't done much good, and I want a second opinion.' Her voice was rising and there was a tremor in it as she said, 'I can't go on like this! I want to see another ear, nose and throat specialist immediately.'

She was becoming aggressive, as if she thought Tessa might refuse the request, and when she said calmly, 'I agree entirely, Mrs Durant. I think you should get a second opinion,' the woman's face crumpled and tears began to flow.

'Thank God for a listening ear!' she gulped.

'If you'll excuse me for a moment, I'll consult Dr Tarrant about who to refer you to,' and, leaving Angela Durant to compose herself, she went to catch Ben between patients.

She hadn't spoken to him since the previous evening, as she'd been almost late, after a sleepless night going over the nightmare meeting in the restaurant. Ben had already been ensconced with his first patient of the day when she had arrived.

What must he think of her? she'd asked herself a hundred times during the small hours of the morning, and what had Miles Callender meant when he'd said that the woman out of Ben's past was in circulation again? Was she separated, divorced, widowed? Whatever it was, Tessa wished she'd stayed away.

It seemed that Ben didn't have that sort of feeling, however. He'd chosen to be with her, to spend some of his precious free time with her, which was more than he'd thought of doing with Tessa, so maybe the flame was still burning.

That was difficult enough to cope with, but for the moment it was the other thing that was so distressing: for him to have to deal with his friend's curiosity at such a traumatic time, a reunion with his ex-fiancée, and for herself to have been with him—a member of the practice. She ached to apologise, to make him believe that she'd known nothing about what Miles was up to, but this wasn't the place, and so when they came face to face, she merely said quietly, 'Good-morning, Ben. I have a patient who wants a second opinion from an ear, nose and throat man, in my opinion with just cause. Who do you recommend?'

'Who's she already seen?' he asked, his face expressionless.

'Bellows.'

'Right, then send her to Alexander Thompson. There's none better.'

'Thanks, I'll do that.'

She hesitated. It was as if her feet were stuck to the floor.

'Is there something else?' he asked.

'Er—no, nothing for now,' she stammered, and made a quick exit.

When she went back into her own room, Angela Durant had got herself under control and was powdering her nose.

'It was so bad after the operation,' she said, 'that I

used to scrape the gunge off the back of my throat myself.'

'What?' Tessa stared at her in horror. 'There could be your answer. You could have damaged the membranes.'

Her patient looked away.

'I was desperate, and in any case, it's their fault if I did. The whole thing was bungled from the start.'

When she'd gone, a woman who was used to being in charge of her life, and not one to suffer fools gladly, apart from her own misdoings, Tessa rang for the next patient and was confronted with a ten-year-old boy and his father.

On asking what the problem was, she was told, 'David played football for the school team last night, and when he came home he said that he'd collided with one of the other boys, head on, and that his head hurt and felt all swimmy inside. And this morning it's no better, Doctor. I'm worried in case there's any damage to his skull,' the father explained.

'And rightly so,' she agreed. 'Come here, David,' she said with a reassuring smile, as the small dark-eyed boy faced her warily.

She felt his head all over and there were no soft swellings to indicate bleeding, and when she looked into his eyes there appeared to be no problem, but when she held up one finger and asked him how many, he promptly replied, 'Two,' and on her presenting three fingers he said, 'Five. . . I think.'

Tessa turned to the father.

'David is showing some degree of double vision. I want you to take him to hospital for tests. I'm going to phone the paediatrician at the infirmary to let him know that you're coming.'

She wrote out a quick note for them to take to the hospital and asked, 'Are you in a car?'

'Yes,' she was told.

'Good. Go right there, then. It's Ward A1. . .and try not to worry. They'll give David a thorough checking over, and if there is any problem he'll be in the right place to have it seen to, and if there isn't. . .well, better to be safe than sorry, eh?'

The morning sped on like any other busy day at the practice, but it wasn't like any other day, was it? Tessa thought miserably. She *must* speak to Ben, make her apologies, offer her explanations, and where normally, in her usual forthright manner, she would already have made the opportunity to do so, in spite of her desperation there was a desire in her to chicken out. Because if in the course of the conversation he should tell her that he and Georgina were on course again, her misery would be endless.

But why would he do that? she asked herself as she tapped on his door at lunchtime. Why should Ben discuss his private affairs with her? What he did with his life was no business of hers. . .unfortunately.

'I'm going to the café for lunch,' she said weakly when he looked up. 'Would you like to join me?'

She could have said that compared with last night it would be slumming, but at the moment she hadn't a joke left in her.

'I can't,' he said tonelessly. 'I want to go home to check on Dad.'

'Oh, I see,' she said lamely, and turned away.

'What is it?' he asked. . .as if he didn't know!

'I need to talk to you away from this place.'

'Come with me, then,' he suggested. 'Mum will rustle up a sandwich for us.'

'Are you sure?' she asked in the same lifeless tone.

'Yes, we can talk on the way.'

'What I have to say won't take long,' she said with an attempt at a smile.

His head jerked up.

'You're not leaving?'

'No, of course not. . .unless I get the push?'

It was Ben's turn to smile and it was a better effort that her own.

'That isn't likely. I've told you—I've got to put up with you if only for your entertainment value.'

'Yes, well, I'm not exactly court jester this morning,' she told him sombrely as she slid into the passenger seat of his car, and if he *was* going to start all over again with the unhappy looking redhead, Tessa didn't feel as if she would ever laugh again.

'So?' he said as they moved out on to the road.

She swallowed.

'It's about last night, Ben,' she began.

'I thought it might be.'

'I want to apologise for any embarrassment I might have caused you. . .and to explain what I was doing there.'

'Well, I'm expecting this to be good,' he said. 'If you're going to tell me it was a coincidence I'd better warn you that I'm not like a pawn-shop—I don't take *everything* in.'

'It *was* a coincidence on my part,' she told him with sweet earnestness, 'but for your friend Miles it was anything but. He rang and asked me out to dinner, and I never dreamt it was because he needed someone at short notice to partner him on his snooping trip. When he told me that you would be arriving any moment with—er—Georgina, I was flabbergasted and would have left, but you were there before I could do so.'

'Miles is like that,' he conceded with a half-smile

'He does things without thinking. That's always been his trouble. The thing that amazes me about all this, though, is the fact that you were prepared to dine with a man that you'd only just met. He rang you up and asked you out, and at the drop of a hat you went with him?'

'Perhaps it was because he was a friend of yours that I trusted him,' she said defensively.

'Or perhaps it was because he was available?' he said with a frown. 'Miles has two divorces behind him. He's a womaniser. Yes, he is a friend of mine, but it doesn't mean I'd trust him with a woman who belonged to me.'

'So?' She was still on the defensive. She'd expected to be shown the extent of his anger, but not to have her morals questioned. '*I* don't belong to you, do I?'

He took his eyes off the road for a second and she saw that his calm was gone; they were a stormy blue, like the angry sea.

'No, you don't! Which is perhaps a good thing, as I'd be tempted to lay you across my knee and wallop your backside if you did.'

'So you wouldn't have cast me off?'

'No.' His face was grim. 'When I make a commitment I keep to it.'

Tessa sighed. The conversation was developing along different lines from what she'd expected, but Ben had just given her an opening and she took it.

'You mean like your commitment to Georgina?'

The farm was ahead of them; in another few seconds they would be there.

'Why bother your head about that?' he said shortly, and before she could think of a reply he had swished to a halt outside the old stone building.

CHAPTER EIGHT

WHEN they got out of the car Tessa said, 'Your neurologist friend isn't likely to be here, is he?'

'No, he saw Dad yesterday, and sadly hadn't any good news for us—not that we were expecting any. You know, whatever impression he might have given you, Miles *is* top of his field. We were at college together, and he was always ahead of the rest of us.'

'He said something similar about you,' she told him.

Ben laughed.

'A mutual admiration society, from the sound of it.'

'Miles thought you should have specialised.'

'So he's always telling me, but I'm content as I am. We GPs have just as important a function at our level as the likes of Miles and his associates, and don't ever let anyone convince you otherwise.'

'They won't. If I'd wanted to do that I would have signed off long ago. As it is, it's taking me all my time to cope at Woodbank.'

'Rubbish! You're doing fine. . .and self-denigration doesn't suit you. I prefer you when you're bumptious.'

He was opening the door to the farmhouse and she replied quickly, 'Yes, but you'd prefer me even more if I had green eyes and auburn hair, or was a leggy blonde.'

He stopped with his hand on the latch.

'You think you've got me all worked out, don't you, Tessa?'

'Haven't I?' she questioned, her cheeks beginning to burn.

'You'll have to wait and see, won't you?'

As they went inside the memory of a dream that she'd had among her tossing and turning of the previous night came to mind. It had been of a wedding in a small village church. The bridegroom had been tall and flaxen-haired, and there had been *three* brides walking down the aisle to meet him, while she had been sitting at the back with the also-rans.

When they went into the sitting-room Ben's mother was seated by the window, and her face brightened when she saw them.

'Ben!' she said. 'And you've brought Tessa again. How lovely to see you, my dear.'

She looked tired and drawn, and Tessa's heart went out to her. Her own parents had died from prolonged illnesses and she could still remember the misery and exhaustion of caring for the terminally sick.

'How's Dad?' Ben asked immediately.

'Sleeping at the moment. The nurse is with him,' and then with soft anguish she said, 'Do you know what I wish, Ben?'

'No. What?' he asked gently.

'That he wouldn't wake up. . .that he could just drift away out of the pain and suffering.'

'He will,' he assured her gravely, 'very soon.' He kissed her smooth cheek gently. 'Until then we have to soldier on, I'm afraid. I'm going up to see him, and while I'm up there, is there any chance of you making us a quick bite, Mum?'

She sprang to her feet immediately.

'Yes, of course,' and to Tessa, 'It is doing the ordinary basic things that keeps me sane. How about a pot of tea, a ham sandwich, and a piece of my fruit-cake?'

'That would be delightful,' Tessa told her, 'and do let me help.'

'Yes, all right,' she agreed, and led the way into the kitchen.

'How are you settling in at the practice?' she asked as she buttered fresh bread and cut juicy slices of home-cooked ham.

Tessa pulled a wry face.

'Not too bad. I'm trying my best, but I've had one or two hiccups. I'm amazed at the workload. I don't know how Ben copes, as the place seems to revolve around him.'

His mother sighed.

'He's fit and very active, and although it grieved me when he had to give up his own place because of us, I've been glad to be here for him with a meal whenever he wants one, and to be able to see that his laundry is done. . . But, you know, Tessa, I'd like to see my son married.'

So would I, Tessa thought. . .to me!

'But it must be to the right one. It is so important when making a choice of partner for life. Ben was engaged once, but it all went wrong, and since then all his women friends have been just that—friends. The woman he was to have married was young and very beautiful. . .and selfish, and I've never regretted her throwing him over.'

She was pouring boiling water into the teapot with a worried frown on her face.

'And what do you think? She's back in the district, staying with her parents at the Old Manor House on Scully Hill. . .and she's free again. Her husband was killed two months ago in a car crash, and I have this horrible feeling that she's after Ben again.'

So have I, Tessa thought, and, depressing though it

was, there was comfort in knowing that Ben's mother shared her dismay.

'I'm sure that Ben won't allow himself to be involved in anything that he doesn't want,' she said gently, and his mother's face lightened.

'Yes, I suppose you're right. He's certainly got a mind of his own, otherwise he would have been married to her in the first place, and he isn't in the habit of making rash decisions.' She eyed the small, brown-haired girl seated at her kitchen table and asked, 'Are *you* promised to anyone, Tessa?'

Tessa smiled. The quaint and rather beautiful way of phrasing the question had made her throat tighten, and she thought it would be easy to say, Yes, I'm promised to someone, but the promises are all on my side, unfortunately.

Instead she said, with a bright smile, 'No, not at the moment, Mrs Tarrant. We junior doctors don't have a lot of time for socialising.'

The older woman laughed.

'No? I would have expected the young men to be queueing up to take out a lovely young girl like you.'

'They're not, I'm afraid,' Tessa told her with a wry smile. 'I'm not very skilled in the art of man-chasing. I'm usually the joker in the pack.'

Ben's mother said smilingly, 'I would have likened you more to one of the beautiful red queens.'

'No, that's Georgina,' Tessa said miserably, and knew immediately that she'd given herself away, but Mrs Tarrant didn't comment. She just smiled thoughtfully and began to pour the tea.

Ben was silent on the way back to the surgery and Tessa didn't intrude upon his thoughts. She'd seen his expression when he came downstairs after seeing his father, and, although he'd eaten the food that his mother had provided, she'd been aware that it was an automatic exercise.

On their outward journey it had seemed as if the most important thing in the world was to clear the air over the previous night, and to try to get nearer to Ben, but now, beside the plight of a dying man, it all seemed very trivial.

When they pulled up outside Woodbank he said soberly, 'Dad's lungs are inflamed. He's heading for pneumonia, but I *have* to treat him.'

Tessa stared at him.

'Well, of course you have.'

He nodded.

'Yes, but although he can't speak his eyes are pleading with me not to, and there is no way I can do as he asks.'

He leaned forward and rested his head on the steering-wheel, saying grimly. 'I wouldn't do it for anyone else, and I can't do it for him, but, oh, Tessa, I wish I could.' His sigh came from deep within him. 'As it is, I shall arrange for him to be given antibiotics intravenously, along with oxygen, and if it becomes necessary, artificial ventilation. Miles and I have already discussed this eventuality and have agreed on the treatment.'

Tessa reached out and put her arms round him. There was no guile in the gesture, just the action of a compassionate friend, and he turned his head and met her tender brown gaze.

'You'd think that we doctors would be able to cope with this sort of thing better than the rest of the population, wouldn't you? But it isn't so. It hurts just as much as anyone else's grief,' he said gravely.

'If it didn't we would be less than the person we want to be,' she said softly, and he smiled.

'Thank you for that, oh, wise one. You never cease to surprise me, Dr Martin.'

'I never cease to surprise myself, Dr Tarrant,' she retorted, and because his lips were so near, and because she loved him so, she kissed him gently on the mouth.

After the first amazed second he kissed her back, and it wasn't gentle any more. Passion flared between them and, oblivious of passers-by, and the fact that the entrance to the surgery was only feet away, they clung to each other in a moment of supreme rapture. . .and then he drew back, quickly, abruptly, as if he'd been caught off guard, and as Tessa's mouth became a soft round O of disappointment, Ben said, 'I've a few problems in my life at the moment, and you, Tessa Martin, are well on your way to the top of the list.' Opening the car door he got out on to the stone forecourt of the practice and calmly waited for her to join him.

When she reached the sanctity of her own small room Tessa touched her lips gently. It had seemed so right out there in Ben's car, so inevitable that they should be in each others arms, but Ben Tarrant was no push-over. He wasn't a limpid-eyed Enrico, or a worldly, womanising Miles Callender. He had a strength and dignity all his own, and if he ever did get round to finding himself a wife, she hoped that he would remember those magical moments in the front of his car.

It was antenatal day once more, and the afternoon sped by with new pregnancies to be confirmed, progressing ones to be monitored, and as she and the community midwife moved among them Tessa resolutely put Ben out of her mind for the moment.

She'd observed Zilla Green in the waiting-room, and when her name was called she appeared, still looking unkempt and wild, and with a thickening waistline. The eccentric artist seemed to have settled into the pregnancy, and when Tessa examined her there were no problems.

As she moved on to the next cubicle, Annabel went to speak to Zilla, and Tessa could hear her questioning her as to whether she needed any financial or physical help.

'No,' she was told. 'I can afford to keep myself with my painting, and *he* helps me out. I've had a scan and I'm not as worried now.'

'Good,' Annabel said, 'and when you say "he", are you referring to the baby's father?'

The wild-haired woman stared at her.

'Who else?'

'He is living with you, then?'

As Tessa continued with her palpitation of a young mother who was twenty weeks pregnant, and noted to her satisfaction that the fundus, the rounded top part of the uterus, had reached the navel, she heard Zilla say irritably, as if she would have expected the questioner to be already aware of the fact, 'No, of course he isn't. He's a sailor. I'm his wife in *this* port!'

Tessa turned away to hide a smile, and the girl she was examining giggled. Zilla Green was a peculiar woman, she thought, yet as one got to know her better there was something likeable about her, even though the mind did boggle at the thought of a child arriving into such a strange set-up, and then, as if to confound her, the unlikely mother-to-be told Annabel, 'I've bought a pram. It's a big Silver Cross. *I'm* not going to push my child around in one of those canvas buggies like the young 'uns do.'

'Good for you,' Annabel replied. 'And remember, Zilla, if you need any help, I'm here, or I can put you in touch with a social worker.'

A large Christmas tree had been delivered in the late afternoon by a local nursery and erected in a corner of the waiting-room. Once the men had gone, Jean Carswell appeared with a large cardboard box of ornaments out of the cupboard in the stock-room and from then on, every time one of them had a second to spare, they proceeded to decorate the tree.

'It will be here before we know it,' Alice said with a rueful smile as she and Tessa hung the delicate glass baubles on the branches of the spruce. 'And I haven't bought a single present yet.'

'Neither have I,' Tessa told her, as she stepped back to admire the effect, 'but I've only two to buy, so it won't take long.'

'And who might they be for?' the practice nurse wanted to know.

She'd been referring to Dominic. . .and Ben, as it seemed the most natural thing in the world to buy a gift for the man she loved at the most celebrated season of the year, but her face warmed as she imagined the expressions of the staff if they were to discover she'd bought a gift for Ben, and so she said coolly, 'For my brother. . .and a friend.'

Jean was nearby and she laughed.

'Lucky you. I've got a list as long as my arm. Frank is one of a family of eight!'

Gaynor didn't say anything, and Tessa wondered what sort of a Christmas was in store for her. Whenever she asked about her son Gaynor clammed up, as if the surprising conversation on Tessa's first day at the practice had never taken place, and Tessa had a gut feeling that the nervous little woman was still under a lot of pressure.

As if Anne-Marie had read her thoughts about the gift for Ben, she said crisply, 'I don't know if you are aware of the fact, but we collect among ourselves to buy each of the partners a gift, and they in return give each of us a cheque.'

'Fine,' she said. 'I'll be only too pleased to contribute,' but I shall still buy Ben a gift from myself, she thought, not only because she cared for him, but because for him the coming festive season would have little joy, with his father so gravely ill.

As she drove home that night along roads that were ablaze with Christmas lights, Tessa was reminding herself that Ben wasn't alone in his pain. He had Georgina to comfort him now, but it didn't alter the fact that her last thoughts before falling asleep on the lumpy bed in Dominic's spare room, were of the two of them in each other's arms. Ben had kissed her as if he meant it. . .but had he? She'd no cause to search her heart for the reason for her own response, but she would give a lot to know what his had meant.

On Saturday night she went to the cinema with Dominic. For once he was at a loose end and he'd suggested they go together, but when they came out he'd chanced across a crowd of his friends *en route* for an Indian restaurant and been anxious to join them.

'Come with us, Tess,' he coaxed, but she'd shaken her head.

'I'm not in the mood,' she had told him. 'But you go ahead. I'm going back to the flat.'

She'd been restless and on edge all evening, and the film had barely registered because she couldn't get Ben out of her mind. He'd looked drawn and tired when they'd left the practice the previous night, and when she'd asked about his father earlier in the day he'd merely said, 'No better, Tessa.'

It was taking all her strength of will not to seek him out, but she felt that he might feel that he saw enough of her during the week without her foisting herself on to him at weekends.

On her way home she had to pass the practice and her eyes widened when she saw a light on inside. Pulling over to the side of the road, she eyed it thoughtfully. Who could be at Woodbank at this time of night? Only the week before, a practice at the other side of the town had been burgled and the computer stolen. Was this another break-in?

There was only one way to find out. Tessa got out of the car, and gripping her key to the back door of the building, she made her way quickly towards it, keeping in the shadows all the time.

The light was coming from the reception area where the computer was kept, and as the door swung open noiselessly her heart was pounding. The only means of self-defence in the car had been a large torch which came in handy on late calls and, as she held it in her hand like a truncheon, she wasn't too clear what she was going to do with it if confronted by an intruder, but its cold weight in her hand was reassuring as she moved towards the door from where the light was showing.

With her hand on the door-handle, she heard the sound of a chair being scraped back, and then footsteps coming towards her, and she froze on the stone-tiled floor of the passage.

When it was flung open there were no balaclava-hooded figures holding menacing weapons framed in it, but Ben. . .and Georgina, and with a sinking heart Tessa thought dismally that she'd interrupted a tête-à-tête once again.

'Tessa! What on earth are *you* doing here?' he asked testily. 'And why are you holding that torch aloft?'

Her hackles rose immediately. She could ask him the same question. In the space of a few seconds she'd been transported from fear to pique and, furious for putting herself in such a position, she quipped, 'It's raining outside and I haven't got an umbrella.'

'Have I to ask you the question again?' he gritted.

'No, I'll come clean,' she volunteered. 'I was on the point of instigating a self-defence exercise.'

'You're still not talking sense,' he said in the same edgy tone.

'I was passing and saw a light on. I thought that a break-in might be taking place.'

If she was expecting a commendation for valour it wasn't forthcoming.

'What?' he growled. 'You ventured in here on your own? Intending to face an intruder, or maybe intruders? Are you crazy? You could have been killed!'

'Yes, well, I wasn't,' she said pertly. 'I'm alive to tell the tale, so no harm's done, is it?' Tessa was conscious that his companion hadn't spoken, and she thought that if Ben did have yearnings for the green-eyed Georgina, it was hardly likely to be her sparkling conversation that was captivating him all over again. She looked the same as the other night, beautiful in a ravaged sort of way. . .and very sombre.

'You can't blame the child for trying to protect the property, Ben,' she said languidly, as if guessing the thoughts of the unexpected arrival. 'She wasn't to know that it was us inside.'

No, she wasn't, Tessa thought in silent agreement,

and if she'd been given the choice, facing a burglar would have been preferable to finding Ben with Georgina.

'I'm sorry about Saturday night,' Tessa said when they met on Monday morning.

Ben was leafing through the post and, looking up briefly, he said, 'Forget it,' in a far milder tone than the one he'd used at their last encounter. 'And will you please stop apologising, Tessa? It doesn't suit you. It was simply that Georgina had been at the farm and I was taking her home. We stopped off at the practice for some paperwork that I needed. . .that's all, and for goodness' sake don't put yourself at risk like that again!'

Tessa eyed him angrily. On the two occasions when she'd stumbled on him with Georgina he'd managed to put *her* in the wrong, when in truth she'd had no idea that she was about to be involved in his affairs.

The first time he'd shrugged off Miles's behaviour, and his own, by making a big thing about her accepting his friend's invitation on such short acquaintance, and now he was harping about the danger if she'd come face to face with an intruder. His concern over her would be delightful if it flowed from the same well as her own feelings, but as it was. . .

'I'm quite capable of taking care of myself,' she told him stonily, thinking of the miserable Sunday she'd just spent imagining him with his ex-fiancée, only to be told that it was merely a practice matter that had taken them to Woodbank at that time of night.

'I don't understand why you were so uptight when I appeared on Saturday night,' she snapped.

'Bricks and mortar, computers and so on, are expendable. You aren't! Do I have to spell it out?'

'Yes, please,' she said guilelessly as her spirits began to rise.

Ben gave a low laugh.

'Well, I'm not going to. You'll have to get that fertile brain of yours working, and figure it out for yourself,' and, turning to the duties of the day, 'I've got some visits to make after morning surgery, and I'd like you to come along.'

'Sure,' she said breezily, and unable to resist the dig, 'It won't be a threesome with Georgina, will it?' Before he could reply she departed to carry out her own functions in the practice, ruefully aware that she'd been sidetracked again. He was an expert at it.

Their first call of the day was at a small top-floor flat in a neat block not far from the surgery, and as they got out of Ben's car he said, 'This one is my favourite patient.'

'I wouldn't have thought you had favourites,' she teased.

'You'll understand why when you meet her,' he told her as he led the way along the corridors incorporating two flights of stairs.

Tessa groaned inwardly as she thought, Please don't let it be another competitor in the 'Who's going to marry Ben Tarrant stakes'!

When he rang the doorbell she could hear slow determined steps moving towards the door, and when it opened, a small wrinkled old lady with bright brown eyes was standing there, leaning heavily on a stick with a special support handle.

Her face lit up when she saw them.

'Dr Tarrant!' she cried. 'Come in. How nice to see you,' and, with a keen glance at Tessa, 'And who's this?'

'My assistant, Dr Martin,' he said with a smile, and

as they followed the old lady into a neat little sitting-room he told Tessa, 'This is Daisy Turner, the toughest ninety-four-year-old you are ever likely to meet.'

'Mr grandson is training to be a doctor,' she said proudly, giving Tessa a warm smile. 'Isn't that great?'

'It is indeed,' she agreed.

'Daisy broke her hip eight weeks ago,' Ben explained, 'and confounded the hospital and everybody else by being on her feet and mobile again within a week of the operation.'

She nodded.

'They all thought I would have to move to a ground floor flat,' she said with a chuckle, 'but I'm managing the stairs just fine. . .and guess what?' she said to Ben.

'I don't know, what?' he said with an answering laugh.

She pointed towards the bedroom where a half packed suitcase lay on the bed.

'I'm off to Llandudno tomorrow with the over-sixties club across the way.'

He frowned.

'And you're happy about that? It can be chilly on the coast at this time of the year.'

'Of course I am,' she beamed. 'The club always go away for a pre-Christmas holiday, and I didn't want to miss it.' She looked across at Tessa. 'They rely on me for the concerts.'

'Daisy is a singer,' Ben explained. 'She has a beautiful voice.'

'Aye, I have,' she agreed without pride, 'and I thank the Lord for it. I'm in big demand for singing at weddings, and I keep telling Dr Tarrant that he'll have to get a move on as I don't know how much longer I've got.'

He patted her hand.

'I've no doubt you'll be around when the time comes,' he assured her easily. 'And now let's have a look at your legs.

'Daisy's legs have been very swollen and discoloured since the operation,' he told Tessa, 'making the skin very taut, and a knock or another fall could be disastrous.'

The old lady was rolling her stockings down, and once they were at her ankles she said triumphantly, 'That didn't take long, did it? And do you know why? I'm wearing pop-socks!'

Her legs were in a poor condition, but Ben seemed pleased to find that there was some improvement, and he said, 'You're still taking the water tablets, aren't you, Daisy?'

'Yes, of course I am, Doctor,' she chirped. 'I'm not a fool. When somebody tells me to take something for my own good, I take it.'

'That's good.' he said. 'Keep on with them, and I'm going to leave another prescription so that you don't run short.'

'I'm a very lucky woman,' Daisy said. 'A new hip at ninety-four, and back on my feet again. When the doctor was sawing away at me in the hospital I told him to make a good job of it as I don't want to pop off yet, not until I've seen my grandson become a fully qualified doctor.'

She glanced at Ben.

'Would you both like a cup of tea?'

'Yes,' he said promptly.

'Well, you know where the kettle is,' she said. 'Give us a shout when it's ready.'

When Tessa got to her feet and offered to do it, Ben said, 'No, Tessa. I always make the tea, don't I, Daisy?'

'Yes, you do,' she agreed, and when Ben had

disappeared into the kitchen she said softly, 'He's a grand man, none better. If I were fifty years younger I'd snap him up.'

'I can see why she's your favourite,' Tessa said, as they drove away with Daisy waving them off from the window.

'It's her spirit that I admire,' he said. 'She brought up two children on next to nothing, waited until they were married, and then left her husband because he beat her. She'd no home, no money, and there weren't any refuges for battered wives in those days. She survived because she's never been afraid of hard work.'

CHAPTER NINE

THERE had been no joy in their next call. James Latimer had Hodgkin's disease. At fifty-five, with a prosperous car sales outlet, a devoted wife, and a large house on Scully Hill near to where Georgina's parents lived, he'd had everything to live for until some months previously; after feeling generally unwell with fever, loss of appetite, and some weight loss, he'd become aware of enlarged lymph nodes in his neck and armpits.

A man who believed that if you ignored something it went away, he hadn't consulted his GP until a dose of flu that he would normally have thrown off had made him so ill that his wife had sent for Ben, who had seen danger signals other than just a bout of influenza.

Once the man had made a prolonged recovery Ben sent him for tests; chest X-rays, a CT scan, and a bone-marrow biopsy had produced devastating results for the Latimers.

James, who had a short fuse at the best of times, was now a bitter shell of a man after months of radiotherapy and anti-cancer drugs.

'What are his chances?' Tessa had asked before they'd entered the house.

'Difficult to say,' Ben had said. 'He *does* have a chance. There's been an improvement in his condition, and now it's wait and see time because he's finished the treatment. He needs to get his strength back, and a change of attitude would help, but he's very bitter about the whole thing.'

'Not like Daisy.'

147

Ben had smiled.

'No, not like Daisy, but she's unique and, let's face it, she's lived almost forty years longer than James Latimer.'

'How are you this morning, James?' he'd asked carefully when the man's wife ushered them into a luxurious conservatory where the patient, who was thin and very pale, was sprawled among a mass of cushions on a cane sofa.

'Worse than yesterday, and no doubt better than tomorrow,' he had growled.

'You're not forgetting that your last scan showed some improvement, are you?' Ben had asked levelly. 'You have to give yourself time now. You need to get your strength back, and then we'll see. To use a phrase that's becoming rather trite, but is good advice nevertheless, think positive.'

As James Latimer had given a disdainful snort, Ben had continued, 'Your wife is very tired too, you know. How about a holiday? I'm sure if you check with the hospital they will agree.'

Molly Latimer's face had lit up at the suggestion, but her husband had snarled, 'Can you see me sunbathing in this state?'

'Most folks on holiday are too busy enjoying themselves to be bothered about anybody else,' Ben had told him. 'Let Molly here go and book you both a couple of weeks in the sun.'

'No way!' he had spat.

'Don't take your misery out on her,' Ben said, his voice hardening. 'She's exhausted. You've been told there is an improvement, and although you're not prepared to believe it, you could start thinking about somebody else besides yourself for a change. For God's sake, take what's being offered, man, and stop being so bloody-minded!'

When he'd finished speaking there had been silence in the room, and Tessa, seeing gratitude in the woman's eyes, had thought that Ben had perhaps said what she in her devotion had hesitated to express.

James Latimer had eyed his wife as if he was seeing her for the first time in months, and he'd rolled over slowly and produced a wallet out of his back pocket. Extracting a credit card from it, he'd held it out to her and said ungraciously, 'Go on, then. Go and get it booked!' As her eyes filled with happy tears, Tessa had thought that Ben was just as proficient at handing out that sort of medicine as he was at prescribing that supplied by the drug companies.

And now it was afternoon and he was ensconced with a representative of one of those same drug companies in the highly competitive world of pharmaceuticals, being told about new products, special offers, and a hundred other things that the keen-eyed rep would have been instructed to impart to every GP who had the time to listen.

Tessa had a couple of hours free and she was going to spend the time doing some Christmas shopping. It was now less than two weeks away, and the excitement and anticipation of the season hadn't yet got to her. In London there had been parties, nights in the pub, the theatre and, no matter how jaded she'd been coming off duty, she'd never been too tired to join in, but this year it was different. She was in a different place, living a different kind of life. She'd made few friends in the months she'd been at Woodbank, apart from the staff, because her thoughts were all centred on one person, and that fact could mean that a lonely Christmas lay ahead of her.

If Dominic thought she was going to be alone he would want her to join him and his friends, but she wouldn't want that. They were too young, too brash and immature, and as she went out into a bleak wind, hugging a long red knitted coat around her, her usual bounce was absent.

For Dominic she chose a silk waistcoat in bright, warm colours, and her gift for Ben, if she ever found the nerve to give it to him, was a cashmere sweater the same colour as his eyes. She would have liked to buy something more personal, but sadly, their relationship to date didn't warrant it, and so the blue sweater it was.

As she walked back to the practice the light was already fading. By the time the last surgery of the day was over, the dark winter night that could be cosy or bleak, according to one's mood, would have cast its mantle over the town, and she would be going home to another evening of chores and television, or prowling around the flat like a tawny young lioness.

When she walked into the waiting-room Tessa was immediately aware of an atmosphere. The receptionists were talking among themselves with sober faces, and Ranjit was hovering, obviously awaiting her return.

'Ben has had to go home, Tessa,' he said agitatedly in his soft broken English. 'His father is worse. We will have to divide his patients between us tonight.'

'Yes, of course,' she agreed, wondering if her melancholy had been the forerunner of this.

The patients were beginning to file in and she looked around her. The only help she could give Ben at this moment was to keep the practice functioning, along with the rest of the staff, and he would most certainly want that. There was no way he would want chaos at Woodbank because his own life was in trauma, and so she said briskly, 'We'd better get cracking then, eh, Ranjit?'

He was more relaxed now, his earlier agitation forgotten, and as they separated to go to their consulting-rooms Tessa was praying that the suffering of Ben's father would soon be over.

As the night progressed Tessa found that the telephone on the coffee-table in the flat was having the same mesmeric effect on her as the buzzer on her desk during the early days at Woodbank.

She wanted desperately to ring Ben, to let him know he was in her thoughts, but it was the knowledge that she would be intruding into the tragedy that was unfolding at the farm that held her back. At times such as this, families needed only each other. That was how it had been when she'd lost her parents, and yet the longing to go to him was so strong it was making her feel ill.

In the end it was an incoming call that had her dashing to lift the receiver, but it wasn't Ben. A husky, unfamiliar voice asked, 'Is that Dr Martin?'

'Yes,' she said abruptly, groaning inwardly at the thought that it might be an emergency coming through, and it was, in an unexpected sort of way.

'This is Georgina, Ben's friend,' the voice said flatly. 'I wonder if you could possibly come over to be with Mrs Tarrant? She is very distressed and doesn't seem to want me around, and to be truthful I don't want to be here myself. I lost my husband a short time ago and do not want to be in contact with death again if I can help it. I thought that another woman, and a doctor at that, would be the ideal person to be with her at this time.'

Tessa's face was stretched in amazement. The summons to the farm that she'd been longing for had come, but from a most unlikely source, the self-centred Georgina! Or was it possible that she might be a reasonable individual who knew when she wasn't wanted, at least by Ben's mother, and instead of taking offence was trying to be helpful by bringing someone else to the farm to be with her?

'Of course I'll come,' she said immediately. 'I would have done before, but I didn't want to intrude at such a time. How is Mr Tarrant?'

'Very low. Ben has scarcely left his side since he got here,' she said in the same expressionless tone. 'And don't worry about intruding. Your name *has* been mentioned. I'll wait until you get here and then I shall go.'

As she drove out to the farm Tessa was puzzling over Georgina's strange telephone call. 'Your name has been mentioned,' she'd said. What was that supposed to mean? She couldn't visualise Ben saying, 'Fetch Tessa.' And when Georgina had mentioned her late husband she'd sounded genuinely upset, but, if that was the case, why was she back in Ben's life so soon?

When she knocked on the door it was opened by the woman who'd been occupying her thoughts, and the moment Georgina saw the small figure on the step she said, 'I'm off. They know that I'm going.'

'Er—yes, I see,' Tessa said, and as she went inside, Georgina got into a car parked at the side of the house and drove away.

In the long night that followed, Tessa made tea, offered a listening ear to Ben's mother whenever she came down out of the sick-room, and generally made herself useful.

When she'd walked through the door that Georgina had left open as she departed, Ben and Miles Callender had been coming down the stairs together and both men had eyed her in surprise.

The neurologist had said softly, 'Well, look who's here, the diminutive and delightful Dr Martin.'

'Hello, Tessa,' Ben had said, and she'd wished there'd been more of a welcome in his voice, but she'd told herself that it was hardly the moment to expect effusive greetings. 'What brings you here?'

'Your friend Georgina asked me to come to be with your mother,' she'd said, and refrained from adding, 'and because I've been worrying about you all night I didn't need to be asked twice.'

'I see,' he had said absently, and to Miles, 'You're welcome to stay the night if you wish. I know there is nothing further you can do for Dad, but it's a bleak night to be travelling back in.'

'No, thanks just the same,' his friend had said easily. 'I have a clinic in the morning, and I'm better getting there from my own neck of the woods.'

'Yes, I understand,' Ben had said levelly and, after they'd watched the other man button himself into a thick camel overcoat, he had picked up his case and wished them a brisk goodbye.

At four o'clock in the morning Ben's father slipped away from them and when he and his mother came downstairs Tessa saw that they were both dry-eyed.

'I have no tears in me at this moment,' his mother said sadly. 'It is what he wanted—what we all wanted, isn't it, Ben?—because there was no other way.'

'Yes, it is,' he said softly, 'and in a little while I think you should get some sleep. Shall I get you a sedative?'

'No, I'll sleep, if only because for the first time in many months I won't be listening out for your father. He doesn't need me any more.'

'I'll come up with you,' Tessa offered, and Mrs Tarrant gave her a weary smile.

'Thank you, my dear, and bless you for being here. But what about you? No doubt you have a busy day ahead of you tomorrow.'

'Once I've seen you settled I'll go,' she said, knowing that Ben's mother was right. If she was to do justice to both their sets of patients she would need to recharge her batteries, if only for a short time.

'You musn't leave at this time of night,' Mrs Tarrant said. 'The bed in the spare room is made up.'

When Tessa came downstairs Ben was standing with his back to her, gazing down into the glowing embers of the fire. At the sound of her step he turned and said, 'I need some fresh air. Walk round the yard with me, eh, Tessa?'

She nodded, and without speaking slipped on the cream wool jacket that had been the first thing to hand as she'd left the flat.

It was a clear, starlit night and a full moon graced the sky like a huge silver Christmas bauble. An icy wind nipped their cheeks, and the soles of their shoes clanked on the cobbles as they went to stand by the big wooden gate that led to the fields.

Tessa knew instinctively that there were no words to make such a grief any easier to bear, and for what seemed an eternity they stood in silence, until at last Ben laid his head against the wooden gatepost and groaned out his anguish, and it was then that she put her arms round him, and the words of comfort—and love—fell from her tongue.

They'd gone back inside at last, and she'd gone into the kitchen to make them both a hot drink to take away death's chill, and the coldness of the night, but when she went back into the sitting-room Ben was slumped across the sofa in an exhausted sleep and, knowing that he needed it more than the drink, she left him as he was and went to check on his mother.

Mrs Tarrant was also sleeping and Tessa decided that now was the moment to depart. Like Miles she had a busy day ahead of her, and like him also, it would be easier to set off from the flat than to wake in the guest room at the farm.

Ben made a brief appearance at the practice the next day, in the middle of making funeral arrangements. In answer to enquiries and condolences from the staff, he told them that his mother was coping very well and looking forward to the arrival of her sister from Harrogate, who was going to take her back with her after the funeral.

Tessa stood apart from the little group clustered around him. None of them knew that she'd been at the farm the night before, and she was hoping that he wouldn't tell them, as she could just imagine Anne-Marie's comments if she found out.

Each time their eyes met, his were giving nothing away, and her own bright brown gaze was challenging him to give her a sign that he remembered those moments beside the farmyard gate, but he was turning away, saying that he must have a quick word with Hugo and Ranjit, and then he would be off.

What about me? Tessa cried silently. Have you nothing to say to me?

It seemed that he had, but they weren't the words she wanted to hear.

'I could have kicked myself for falling asleep like that,' he said in a low voice as the others dispersed. 'Why didn't you stay? You put yourself at risk again.'

'I went home for the same reason Miles did. It was

easier to start the day from my own home base. As for being at risk, I'm not a child, Ben, even though I'm frequently treated like one. If you must know, I was called out only half an hour after getting back from your house.'

His face tightened.

'Where to?'

'The abattoir. One of the butchers had nearly chopped his finger off and was refusing to go to hospital.'

'Exactly! That's where he *should* have been taken, instead of you being called out at that hour!' he snapped. 'It's in a very seedy part of the town.'

She smiled her impish smile.

'I got a side of beef out of it.'

'You what?'

'I'm only joking. I wouldn't know what to do with it if I had!'

He smiled and touched her cheek gently.

'There's only *you* could amuse me on a day such as this,' he told her, and went to seek out the other partners.

Tessa gazed after him ruefully. She didn't want to be complimented on her comic capers. She'd been waiting to know what he thought of being told in a cold farmyard that he was her dear love, her darling Ben. . . among other endearments that had come straight from the heart.

Snow fell on the day of the funeral and continued to fall periodically over the next few days and, as the night of the practice Christmas outing drew near, it lay in a thick white carpet over the countryside.

Ben's mother had gone to Harrogate with her sister immediately the funeral was over, and he was alone at the farm. He'd been away from the practice for two days—the day of his father's death, and the day of the funeral—and as the surgeries were full of coughs and colds and other seasonal complaints, Tessa was grateful to have him back again.

He was his usual quiet decisive self, and, though she more than anyone knew the extent of his raw grief, he didn't let it interfere with the service he offered his patients.

There had been no mention of those moments when she'd held him close and poured out her love for him, and Tessa had resigned herself to the fact that either he'd been too distraught to realise she cared or, if it *had* registered with him he'd decided that the best way to deal with an embarrassing incident was to ignore it.

Visions of him alone at the farm with Georgina tormented her, and whenever she thought about the other woman's strange phone call on the night of his father's death, Tessa found it hard to understand how she could just walk away and leave him at such a time, and she wondered how he'd felt about that.

Georgina had been labelled as selfish in the past, and her recent behaviour would seem to come under the same description, and yet she'd taken the trouble to see that Ben's mother had another woman's support when she'd needed it.

On the two occasions she'd seen them together there hadn't seemed to be any animosity in him towards his ex-fiancée, and yet he hadn't exactly been drooling over her either, and Tessa would have given a lot to know just how much it did mean to him to have the grieving, or not so grieving, widow back in his life.

The other partners would be taking their wives to the Christmas get-together at the Highwayman, and if

Ben turned up with Georgina that would be the death-knell to Tessa's hopes.

The day in question dawned bitterly cold. What had been fluffy white snow was now grey ice, and the patients were left with no choice but to struggle to the surgery along glacier-like roads and pavements.

'It's bad up near the farm,' Ben said, as he took off a sheepskin jacket to reveal that he'd discarded more formal wear for a thick Arran sweater and cords. 'The snow is still thick up there. A veritable winter wonderland, as long as one doesn't have to drive in it!'

As usual, the staff had congregated in the kitchen before the day's fray, and as she warmed her hands around a cup of tea Tessa was conscious of Ben's eyes upon her. Her cheeks were glowing with the cold. The chill wind outside had whipped her hair into a tangled halo round her face, and there was nothing in his appraisal to enlighten her as to whether he thought she looked a mess or otherwise.

His mind was obviously on the day ahead as he told them all briskly, 'If any of you want to visit the hairdresser this afternoon, or do some shopping, feel free to do so, as long as you arrange it among yourselves,' and with his gaze back on her, he told Tessa, 'I'll see to it that you have the afternoon free to do the same, Tessa.' Which made her think that maybe she *did* look a mess, but the offer was welcome as she'd already decided that she was going to abandon her harum-scarum image and have her hair done in a more elegant style.

'I have an appointment with my father's solicitor immediately after morning surgery,' he told her, 'but it shouldn't take long, and once I'm back I'll make any visits and keep my eye on the various clinics. The afternoon will be yours.'

He went on to say to them all, 'I suggest that, as we all appear to have brought a change of clothes with us, we make our separate ways to the Highwayman and meet again there. Any questions?'

It appeared that there weren't and, as Anne-Marie went to open the main door to let the patients in, another day at Woodbank was under way.

Tessa made a quick phone call to the hairdresser before summoning her first patient, and was told they could fit her in mid-afternoon, which was exactly what she'd hoped for. Normally she would have washed her hair herself, towelling it and leaving it to dry naturally, but tonight she wanted to look different, and was going to ask them to take it back off her face and to blow it into silken ringlets to fall on her shoulders.

She'd thrown her budget to the winds and bought an expensive shift dress in heavy oyster silk from an exclusive boutique in the town, and intended to wear a gold belt with it and matching jewellery, with the idea in mind that if she didn't make an impact on Ben tonight. . .she never would.

Two o'clock came, with just three-quarters of an hour to her hair appointment, and Ben wasn't back. She'd already been out on four calls, one to an elderly man in an old people's home. He'd had bronchitis that was bordering on pneumonia, and she'd told the staff to keep him as upright as possible, give him plenty of nourishing liquids, and had prescribed Vibramycin, while warning them that admission to hospital was a strong possibility if he became any worse.

The second call had been to Zilla Green, who was complaining of vomiting and discomfort. The door had been opened by a small grizzled man with faded blue eyes and a limp, and as he'd taken her upstairs Tessa had thought that anything less like a jolly Jack-tar she was never likely to see, *if* he was the baby's father.

After a meticulous examination she was able to tell Zilla that all was well. The problems she'd been having were due to the baby having moved.

'It moves all the time!' she'd protested.

'I know that,' Tessa had told her, 'but at seven months you can expect changes of position, and they can cause the mother to feel very strange and uncomfortable until the baby has settled into its new posture.'

The man had stood silent during the examination, and as Zilla hadn't asked him to leave the room Tessa was pretty sure he must be the father. It was still without speaking that he escorted her to the door when she was leaving, and she concluded that he was adopting the policy of least said soonest mended.

The last two calls had been gastric infections, similar to a bug that was going around, and after satisfying herself that neither patient was in any danger, she had settled down to wait for Ben.

While she was watching the minutes tick by, Anne-Marie put a call through and when she lifted the receiver a shrill youthful voice said in her ear, 'My mum wants you to come to see to our Doreen. She's got milk fever. She's on the floor and can't get up, an' my Dad's not here.'

'Who are you?' Tessa asked, breaking into the garbled message.

'Emma Cotter from Cotter's Farm.'

'And you say that Doreen has got milk fever? How long is it since she gave birth?'

'This mornin'.'

'This morning!' Tessa repeated. 'She is hardly likely to have anything like that yet. Who attended her?'

'My mum.'

Tessa's eyes widened. Either she was dealing with some sort of do-it-yourself hillbillies, or the child had got the message wrong, and she asked quickly, 'Where are you ringing from?'

'I'm at home.'

'Yes, I know that, my dear,' she said patiently, 'but where is that? Where is the farm?'

'You know the Tarrant farm?' the child asked.

'Yes, I do indeed,' she said wryly.

'Well, ours is a mile farther on along the same road. Please come,' she begged. 'I don't want Doreen to die!'

'Tell your mother that someone will be on their way within the next five minutes,' she said reassuringly, and, as Ben hadn't come back, Ranjit was out on his calls, and Hugo had gone home to rest before the evening's festivities, she didn't have to make two guesses as to who it was going to be.

Grabbing her coat off the peg and picking up her case, she was calculating that if she got a move on she might be back in time for the hairdresser, and if she wasn't, well, too bad. A sick young mother was more important than her own appearance, but where was Ben? He should have been back ages ago.

As she flew out of the surgery and jumped into her car, Tessa saw that it was snowing again, and as she left the town behind and drove into open country it was clear that it had been coming down for some time there, and that, on top of the snow that Ben had described earlier, was making it difficult to drive.

When she got to the Tarrant farm she was hoping that he might be there, so that she could pass the call on to him and go back to do her own thing, but when she banged on the door and peered through the window there was no sign of him, and with a resigned sigh she continued on her way.

A hundred yards further on, the wheels stuck in the snow, and no matter how she revved the engine the car wouldn't budge, and so, knowing she had no other choice, Tessa picked up her case and got out to walk, grateful that the Cotters' farm was only a mile away in the swirling white wilderness.

She found to her cost that a mile in those conditions wasn't a quick mile, and it was with a sigh of relief that she spotted a chimney first and then a scatter of farm buildings. Thank God she'd arrived! Time to worry about getting back later.

'Who're you?' a small harassed-looking woman asked when she opened the door in answer to her knock.

'Tessa Martin, the newest member of the practice,' she said, as she stamped her feet to loosen the snow on her boots.

'Oh, I see. Well, come on, then,' she said impatiently. 'I'll take you to her,' but instead of leading the way into the house she came outside and led the way to a large shed at the back of the farm and said flatly, 'She's in here.'

Tessa stared at her.

'Why isn't she in the house?'

The woman gave a short laugh and said, 'Nay, I might be worried sick about her, but I can't see Doreen tucked up in bed, somehow. She's there. . .see for yourself,' and she pointed to a black and white cow lying motionless on the hay.

Tessa's mouth dropped open.

'That's Doreen?'

'Yes. Why? What did you expect? Surely Bob Jameson put you in the picture?'

'No,' she said weakly, 'he didn't, and who's Bob Jameson?'

'The vet, of course. I thought you said you were his new assistant.'

'Mrs Cotter,' Tessa said slowly. 'I am a doctor, not a vet. Your daughter rang asking for help at the practice where I work. She was upset, and the message somewhat confused, but I can assure you that I came out here expecting to attend a young mother with a breast-milk problem. . .not a cow!'

She wanted to cry, And I've struggled through snow-drifts to get here. My feet are like ice, and I've missed my hair appointment, and worst of all, Ben will kill me for rushing out of the surgery without the patient's records, and for not telling anyone where I was going. The humiliating thing about all this is that if I *had* gone to look for the records of Doreen Cotter I wouldn't have found any, and it would have made me stop and think.

'You mean that our Emma rang the wrong number?'

'Yes, it would appear so,' she said wearily.

'The stupid child! Although I have to admit that the vet's number and the doctor's are next to each other in my notebook.'

There was only the slightest tremor to indicate that the cow was alive, and Tessa questioned the woman carefully.

'Your daughter said that she'd just given birth.'

'Aye, had a calf this morning, her fourth, but it must have caused a big calcium deficiency. It does that sometimes when they've had a few, and it's dangerous for the cow. We can get injections for this sort of thing from the chemist and I gave her one as soon as she went down, but it needs the vet here to inject calcium right into the vein, otherwise we might lose her.'

Tessa's face was grave as she told her, 'As you can imagine, I don't carry that sort of thing with me, and if that is what's required there is little I can do.'

At that moment the phone rang and the farmer's wife dashed into the house to answer it. When she came back there was a relieved smile on her face.

'That was my husband,' she said. 'He's been to see his mother, who's not at all well. She lives in one of the hill villages, and he left earlier than he intended because of the weather. He's actually at the vet's now. He called in to have word with him about Doreen, and now he knows what's happened he's bringing him along to attend to her. They'll be here in a matter of minutes.'

'Will they be able to get through?' Tessa asked.

'Yes. They shouldn't have any trouble. They'll be in the Land Rover, and it's not as bad on the side they're coming from.'

Tessa was sharing her relief. The problem was solved. Doreen was going to get the correct treatment instead of hit-and-miss attention from a trainee GP. She could go now, get back to her car, and she didn't intend wasting any time with the weather as it was.

'Let me get you some food,' the woman offered, but shaking her head she said,

'No, thanks. I've had to abandon my car. I must get back to it. . .and to civilisation,' and with a brief farewell Tessa set off back down the road.

CHAPTER TEN

GETTING to the Cotters' farm had been traumatic enough, but going back was a nightmare. The snow was so deep by now that every step was an effort and Tessa was wishing that she'd accepted the offer of some refreshment, as with food inside her she would have been warmer and able to move faster.

They would find her body in the snow, she thought wretchedly, as she staggered on, and eventually a brass plaque would be unveiled on the surgery wall in her memory, with always a vase of fresh roses on a shelf beneath it, explaining that she'd died in the course of duty. . .and Ben would spend a lifetime of regret for not having realised her true worth.

So mesmerised was she by the thought of her sacrifice and the effort to keep going, that she didn't see a dark figure loom up in front of her in the blinding snow, until urgent hands gripped her wrists.

'Tessa!' Ben's voice said. 'What are you doing out here?'

Her face crumpled.

'I answered a call to Cotter's Farm.'

'Yes, so I believe. I'd called back at the house for something and Anne-Marie phoned through to say that she thought that was where you'd gone, but that you hadn't taken the patient's records with you.'

He was half carrying her the last few yards to his parents' home. 'And when I saw your car out there almost buried in the snow, I couldn't believe that you would do anything so stupid and irresponsible as to

visit a patient without records and without notifying
the rest of the staff of your whereabouts!'

A lump came up in her throat as the vision of the
touching memorial faded beneath his anger, and she
turned her face away from him. He was supporting her
with one hand and opening the door with the other,
and when the welcoming warmth of the house met her
she wrenched herself out of his arms and slumped on
to the nearest chair, closing her eyes as she did so.

'As the snow was getting thicker and thicker I was
planning my memorial,' she said tonelessly, 'but now it
seems. . .'

'What?' he barked, taking a bottle of brandy out of
the wine cabinet. 'That fools don't warrant memorials?'

She was too cold and humiliated to answer back, and
he didn't know the worst yet. . .that she'd rushed out
of the practice to visit a cow, but, being Tessa, she had
to get it off her chest.

'The young girl who phoned asked me to go to see
Doreen who they thought had milk fever,' she said
raggedly.

'And?'

'Doreen was a cow.'

If he laughed she would die, she thought wretchedly,
but it wasn't amusement that was stretching his face. It
was outraged disbelief.

'You're telling me that you rushed out of the surgery
like a bull in a china shop for a wrong call?'

'Very appropriate,' she giggled feebly. 'A bull dashing after a cow.'

Ben's face became even tighter.

'I can't believe I'm hearing this,' he said coldly,
thrusting a glass of brandy at her. 'You're even making
a joke of it.'

'It will be even more of a joke when the rest of the staff get to hear of it,' she said glumly.

It seemed as if she couldn't get *anything* right as he snapped, 'I'm not in the habit of tittle-tattling about my partners with the rest of the staff——' and glaring at the brandy which was still in her hand untouched '—and drink that!'

'No,' she said defiantly. 'I don't like brandy.'

'It. . .is. . .to. . .warm. . .you. . .up,' he said slowly, as if talking to a child. 'Do I have to pour it down your throat, or do you *want* pneumonia?'

He was moving towards her menacingly, and Tessa lifted the glass to her lips and drained it, thinking that her cool, collected trainer had been replaced by an unreasonable stranger.

As the brandy warmed her blood, so it fired her anger, and now it was her turn to say her piece.

'I'm sick of having the rules and regulations of your precious practice rammed down my throat every time I put a foot wrong,' she flared. 'I know that I've behaved like an idiot again, but everything I do is with the best intentions, and one moment you're patting me on the back, and the next you're knocking me down. What is more, it's your fault I got involved in this. You said you'd be back soon and you weren't. I'd arranged to have my hair done, and now I'll have missed the appointment, and as you're such a stickler for doing the right thing, what did you expect me to do when the call came through, ignore it?'

'I would have expected you to go and get the patient's notes,' he said equably, as if her anger had banished his own. 'It's just a simple practice rule— never visit patients without their notes, and, as we are both now well aware, there isn't a Doreen Cotter on our lists.'

'You don't have to rub it in!' she cried, and, as her anger increased, 'I think Georgina had a lucky escape from you, and she's a fool coming back for more. What you deserve is. . .Anne-Marie. You deserve each other, two clever-clogs together!'

He gave an incredulous snort.

'If you were as good at keeping the practice rules as you are at trying to organise my life, there would be none to beat you. What gives you the idea that I want *any* woman?'

'Exactly!' she said, her voice breaking. 'If you'd held me close out there in the snow and offered some comfort I would have been eternally grateful, but no, not you. All I get is a ticking-off.'

His face was white and set, and yet she'd never seen his eyes more brilliant as he said softly, 'You mean, like this?' and he moved swiftly across the carpet, yanked her up out of the chair and kissed her until she thought her lungs would burst.

When he released her she leaned against him limply and, looking down on her unsmilingly, he said softly, 'Well?'

'Yes, I meant exactly that,' she whispered, 'but with tenderness, not in the form of a punishment.'

He eyed her calmly for a moment and then left the room without speaking. When he returned a few minutes later he said curtly, 'I'll take you home. Your car is still half buried in the snow. I'll dig it out tomorrow. If you don't feel up to coming to the meal tonight, give it a miss.'

'I don't want to go home,' she hissed. 'I want to go to the hairdresser's to see if they'll give me a later appointment, and I *will* be coming to the meal tonight. If you think that a few minor problems such as being caught in a blizzard, almost having to stand in for the local vet, being verbally annihilated by my boss and then ravished by him, are going to flake me out. . . you're mistaken!'

He was laughing now.

'Ravished! That's a bit strong for someone who just melted in my arms.'

He was holding the door for her to go through it, and once she was outside and settled in his car she looked up at him stonily.

'Don't flatter yourself, Dr Tarrant.'

The receptionist at the hairdresser's nodded sympathetically as Tessa explained her reason for not keeping the earlier appointment.

'I'm a doctor, and I was called out to a patient,' she told her, putting the painful connotations of the episode to the back of her mind for the time being.

'Not to worry,' the girl said. 'We can fit you in now. Carlo will attend to you. Have you any style in mind?'

Tessa frowned. The regal ringlet style had lost its appeal since her fracas with Ben. She felt miserable and of no consequence, and if she *was* feeling a nonentity it was Ben's fault. As sudden rebellion rose in her, she said calmly, 'Yes. I'd like it done in dreadlocks.'

'I'll take your late surgery,' Ben had said when he'd dropped her off at the hairdresser's. 'It will give you time to calm down,' he'd pointed out drily, and she'd stiffened in the seat beside him. 'I'll also take you and bring you back,' he'd offered, 'as you've no car.'

'Dominic will take me,' she'd said immediately, blocking the offer.

To her intense irritation, he'd said offhandedly, 'Suit yourself. If you want your brother to take you to the Highwayman, fair enough, and I'll see you home.'

'Maybe,' she'd said capriciously and flounced off into the salon.

When Dominic saw her hair his eyes popped and he gave a low whistle of approval, but his next remark took the edge off it.

'What's old Tarrant going to say about *that*?'

'I've no idea, and I couldn't care less,' she flung back, 'and don't call him old, Dominic. There's not that much difference in our ages.'

He'd eyed her curiously and commented, 'And it wouldn't make you any less keen on him if there was, would it?'

'No,' she admitted. 'It wouldn't, but at the moment I'm well and truly off Ben Tarrant.'

'Why?'

'Because he tore a strip off me this afternoon.'

'What for?'

She couldn't meet his eyes as she told him slowly, 'I went to visit a patient this afternoon, right out in the hills, by the name of Doreen Cotter, and the lady in question turned out to be a cow.'

As she watched his face crumple, Tessa knew that if Ben had controlled his mirth at her mistake, there would be no such luck with her brother and the surmise was correct.

'I don't believe it!' he hooted. 'You knucklehead!' and as he rolled about with laughter Tessa found herself joining in, and as the pair of them split their sides, the afternoon's catastrophe didn't seem quite so bad.

Because Dominic had been dawdling around the flat before they left, Tessa was the last to arrive at the Highwayman restaurant and country club, and when she walked into the bar area the rest of the company were already seated there awaiting her arrival.

Surprisingly, the dreadlocks suited her. Dominic had told her that she looked like a miniature Cleopatra, and to beware of Romans bearing gifts, whereupon she'd told him gloomily that if he was referring to Ben Tarrant, the only thing that he was likely to be offering was her notice.

When the small figure with the exquisitely plaited tendrils hanging around her face appeared in the doorway, there was amazement on the faces before her, and she heard Anne-Marie say scornfully, 'What next?'

But Jean came across and said, 'You look divine, Tessa. Like a small golden goddess,' and Tessa gave her a grateful hug. It had all seemed quite in order when she'd let her pique rule her head and told the hairdresser she wanted dreadlocks, but even though the effect was stunning, it hadn't stopped her from being aware that she'd behaved childishly, and if she did want Ben to tell her she'd outstayed her welcome at Woodbank she was going the right way about it.

Tessa found that she was seated next to him at the meal and wished she wasn't, and yet perversely she was delighted to see that he hadn't brought Georgina. Observing him out of the corner of her eye as he chatted to Mrs Patel on the other side of him, she wondered if he felt the same at being placed next to her.

When he did turn his attention to her they were already on the main course, and by that time, instead of being annoyed at being seated beside him, she was chagrined at being ignored, but his first words to her made up for it. . .in part.

'You look very beautiful,' he said gravely, 'though I'm not sure how you'll go down with the patients.'

'I expect the patients to accept me for what I am,' she said coldly, 'not how they expect me to be, like you.'

He inclined his head unsmilingly as if politeness demanded that he put up with her peculiarities, and said casually, 'Yes, well, we'll have to see, won't we?' and when her face didn't lighten, 'Have you recovered from this afternoon?'

'Yes, of course,' she replied stiffly.

'So it's *all* forgotten?'

What was that supposed to mean? she wondered. Was he asking if his kiss was forgotten, too? But he knew better than that, didn't he? because she'd melted into his arms like a pliable, adoring little robot, and that after he'd just wiped the floor with her. Well, it wouldn't happen again. If she had to date every one of Dominic's friends, Enrico, the pushy Miles Callender, and Uncle Tom Cobbleigh and all, she would get Ben Tarrant out of her system, and as the evening progressed, she behaved as she meant to go on by keeping well out of his way.

While she'd been jiving with the others on the dance-floor, Ben had been chatting to his partners and their wives, but towards the end of the evening he sought her out and propelled her to a table at the side of the room.

'How are you feeling?' he asked, his eyes raking her tight face.

'Physically or mentally?' she asked stonily.

'Both, I suppose,' he countered.

'Physically, very tired. Mentally, still seething at the way you couldn't have cared less whether I got lost in the snow this afternoon. The only thing bothering you was the running of your beloved practice.'

His face was expressionless.

'So that's what you think?'

'Yes, it is,' she told him rebelliously. 'As I was fighting my way through the blizzard, I'd already got you worked out for a lifetime of regret if I died out there, because of your misjudgement of me.'

Blond brows rose in amused amazement as he eyed her stormy face, and he said, 'I'll have to do something about it, then, won't I? As I can't stomach the thought of a lifetime of regret ahead of me.'

'I know that you're making fun of me,' she said, 'but I don't care.'

'That's funny. I thought you did.'

'What?'

'Care.'

Her face went scarlet. So he *had* been aware of the endearments she'd whispered as she'd held him close in the farmyard.

'That's past tense, I'm afraid,' she snapped.

'It didn't seem like that this afternoon when I was— er—ravishing you.'

There was no snappy answer to that, and happily, or unhappily, as the case might be, she was saved from having to make one as Anne-Marie was bearing down on them purposefully, and getting to his feet, Ben murmured, 'We've arranged to have the next dance. Excuse me.'

For the remainder of the night Tessa continued to keep out of his way, but there was no avoiding him when it was time to go. He'd said he was taking her home, and when she went to get her wrap from the cloakroom he was beside her.

'Are you ready?' he wanted to know.

'Yes,' she said briefly.

'Good. We'll say our goodbyes, then,' which they did, and if any of the other members of the party were curious about the arrangement, they had to accept that as Tessa's car was stuck in a snow-drift, it was the logical solution to her getting home.

They drove in silence for the first couple of miles and Tessa was content for it to be so. No words were better than the wrong ones, and she felt that nothing she might say would be right.

It was Ben who broke the silence. He glanced at her set face and said quietly, 'I feel that I ought to explain why I was so late getting back this afternoon.'

'There's no need,' she told him lifelessly.

'Yes, there is,' he argued, his voice hardening. 'I'd commissioned a piece of jewellery to be made, and when I called to collect it at a jeweller's in the town, they couldn't find it. I had to wait while they virtually ransacked the place.'

'I see.'

'I doubt it, but to continue, they did find it in the end on the finger of one of the assistants. She'd been admiring it, tried it on, and then forgotten all about it.'

'So it was a ring?'

Ben smiled.

'That is what one usually wears on one's finger.'

True enough, she thought dejectedly, but whose finger was it destined for?

He was watching her expression, and when there was no joy to be had from her, he changed the subject, asking politely, 'Have you anything planned for Christmas?'

The answer to that was No, nothing, but she wasn't going to tell him *that*.

'Yes, lots of things,' she told him airily. 'It will be a case of trying to fit them all in.'

'Good for you,' he said drily.

She had to ask.

'What about you?'

'Well, for one thing, I shall be spending it at the farm. My mother is quite happy to spend Christmas in Harrogate, and in the circumstances I think it's a good idea. They want me to join them, but I don't think so. There is something I want to resolve at this end.'

I'll bet there is, she thought dismally. He wouldn't have had the ring made for nothing.

'Have you any parties planned?' she asked in morbid self-torture.

'A few,' he said casually. 'Georgina's folks have asked me round.'

'Well, they would, wouldn't they?' she said mockingly.

He ignored the interruption and went on, 'And one or two other folks have issued invitations, so like yourself I shall be kept occupied.'

Yes, occupied putting the ring on her finger, no doubt, she thought bleakly, and wondered what on earth she was doing making polite conversation when they could be making love, *if* they weren't at logger-heads, *and* Ben had kissed her earlier in the day because he wanted to, and not to put her in her place.

In spite of her yearnings, Tessa's hand was reaching for the door-handle the moment Ben stopped the car outside the flats.

'Hold on a minute!' he said quickly. 'You can relax. I only ravish once a day.'

'Very funny,' she hissed.

'I just want to pass on a message, that's all. I've been

debating whether to tell you all evening, as you're in such a prickly mood, but I think I ought to pass it on.'

She eased herself back into the seat reluctantly.

'Pass what on?'

'They rang through from Cotter's Farm just before I left the surgery tonight to enquire if you'd got back all right, and to say that—er—Doreen. . .was much better.'

In the shadows of the car she could just make out the outlines of his face and could tell by the way he was pursing his lips that Ben was holding back amusement. Ignoring the fact that she herself had already had a good laugh at the afternoon's fiasco, she said glacially, 'I see that you've managed to stop thinking about surgery protocol for long enough to decide that it's funny. Well, maybe it was. The whole thing was ridiculous. . .like me!' And opening the door, she flung herself out of the car and whizzed up the path and into the flat before Ben had time to catch his breath.

During the last few days to Christmas it was business as usual at the Woodbank practice. On the morning after the staff outing, Tessa found Gaynor waiting for her in the parking area outside the surgery, and the timid little woman eyed her in surprise when she arrived on foot.

'My car is still snow-bound unless Ben has had time to dig it out,' she reminded her. 'I've come by bus.'

'I wanted to have a word with you before the others arrive,' Gaynor said, with a quick glance around her to make sure they wouldn't be overheard.

'Fire away, then,' Tessa told her, dredging up a smile. 'It looks as if we're the first here.'

'It's about my son, Tessa. I just wanted you to know

that he's back at college and has recovered from the addiction.'

'Why, that's marvellous!' she exclaimed. 'I'm so happy for you both. I've been a bit concerned as you didn't seem to want to talk about it when I've asked you, and I wondered if things were worse.'

Gaynor's own smile was wistful.

'Yes, I know. It was just that I was so worked up about it, that after plucking up courage to tell you that first time, I couldn't bear to mention it again, but now it's almost over I *can* talk about it. . .and thank you for listening, Tessa.'

'I was only too pleased to help in what way I could,' Tessa told her. 'It was such a shame that it should have happened, for both your sakes, for if he hadn't been ill in the first place he wouldn't have got hooked on the amphetamines. How's the narcolepsy?'

Gaynor's face clouded.

'They're not sure that it was that now. The hospital are saying that it might have just been a massive vitamin deficiency.'

Tessa frowned.

'I can't see them making that kind of an error, but that makes it even more sad.'

'Yes, it does, and I'm not going to leave it at that, but at the moment he's fit and well and neither of us could have asked for a better Christmas present.'

'No, indeed,' she agreed, and as Jean and Alice appeared they all went inside to the warmth of the kitchen.

'If you hadn't been in such a rush to get away last night, I was going to tell you that I'd pick you up this morning,' Ben said in a low voice voice when he arrived some minutes later.

'I was quite happy to use public transport.'

'Yes, I'll bet you were,' he said grimly. 'Anything rather than co-operating with me. Well, you can't visit your patients by bus, and so as soon as surgery is over we'll put everything on hold and go to pick up your car. I've dug it out, and providing the engine is working you can drive it back here while I follow on behind.'

'Yes, all right,' she agreed reluctantly, not wanting to be in such close proximity so soon after the previous day's arguments, but she needn't have worried. As they drove out to his parents' place, apart from asking briefly if she'd enjoyed the previous night's gathering, he talked only of practice matters, and she did likewise.

She told him politely that she'd enjoyed herself the night before, but it was far from the truth. She'd been too strung up to get any pleasure out of the occasion. . .and it was *his* fault. . .and that of a meek black and white cow, that thankfully was now on the way to recovery.

After looking forward to the outing which she'd known might be her only really festive occasion over the Christmas holidays, she and Ben between them had spoiled her evening. And now she only needed her car to refuse to start to create an all-time low.

Thankfully, it didn't let her down, and once she was surgery-bound, with Ben following her in his car, Tessa was able to congratulate herself that at least one thing had gone right.

On Christmas Eve there was to be just one surgery in the morning. Once it was over, there would be calls to make, and then they would be free for the next two days, as any emergencies would be dealt with by a central control.

Ben had already finished, and gone out visiting, by the time that Tessa's last patient of the day appeared in answer to the buzzer.

The first thing she noticed about Jack Walsh was that he'd been drinking, even though it was only half-past eleven, and the second was that he was in a temper.

'Where is he, then?' he snarled, the moment he staggered into the room.

'Where is who?' she asked carefully.

'Tarrant, of course.'

'*Dr* Tarrant is out on his rounds,' she told him in the same level tone.

'*Is* he?' He lurched forward, and, breathing alcohol fumes over her, leaned across the desk. 'You'd better go and get him, then.'

'And why should I have to do that, Mr Walsh, when I'm here to help you?'

'What? A bit of a girl! I want to see Tarrant. He's going to pay for meddling in my affairs.'

'I'm afraid I'm not with you,' she told him, trying to keep calm.

'He's told the wife to leave me. That's what he's done! She's taken the family and gone into one of them refuges.'

'You mean, for battered wives?'

The phrase seemed to increase his fury and he grabbed the front of her jacket and pulled her towards him, lifting her off the seat.

'Take your hands off me!' she ordered, but he wasn't prepared to loosen his grip.

'You sound as if you know all about it. In on it with him, are you?' he growled.

'No, of course not,' she gasped, trying to get out of his grasp. 'I'm not in on anything, and as for Dr Tarrant, he would only give that sort of advice in very desperate circumstances.'

'You're all the same, you doctors! Stickin' up for each other, and interferin' in other folks' business.'

Tessa decided that she'd had enough.

'If you don't take your hands off me, I shall call for help and the police will be brought in.'

'You'll do no such thing, madam,' he threatened, and his fist came up and struck her in the face. He was a thick-set man and it was a hard blow that made her sag at the knees. When he saw what he had done, the man loosened his grip, and as he did so she crashed to the ground. With a smothered oath he made for the door, and as blackness descended upon her, Tessa heard the sounds of a scuffle outside, and breaking glass, and the thought came into her mind that there might be a plaque on the wall in her memory after all.

CHAPTER ELEVEN

'You're not going to be looking your best over Christmas, I'm afraid,' the doctor in Casualty told her. 'A couple of black eyes, a nasty cut on the head, and swollen lips, are what Santa's brought for you, my dear.

'That was some smack he gave you, and on top of it you banged your head when you fell. However, the X-rays show that there's no bleeding, and you don't appear to be suffering from double vision, so that's good. When I've stitched that cut, I think we'll have you tucked up in bed in one of the wards for the night, just to be on the safe side.'

'But it's Christmas Eve!' Tessa protested.

'Don't I know it?' he said with a wry smile. 'Once the revelries start, they'll be arriving in droves. Thank God I'm off at New Year.'

'We have a nice line in flannelette nighties,' the nurse who was assisting him said with a smile, and when Tessa grimaced, the doctor eyed her thoughtfully.

'Who do you live with?' he asked. 'I'd let you go home if I knew there was to be a responsible person with you during the night, but unless that's the case you're better off in here.'

She could see the flannelette looming.

'I live with my young brother, and I wouldn't know where to get hold of him as he has a round of parties planned.'

'What about the lady who brought you here?'

'That was Jean Carswell, one of the receptionists from the practice, but she has a husband and family to see to. That's why I insisted she go home. After all, as I've just said, it *is* Christmas Eve.'

'I'll take charge of Dr Martin,' Ben's voice said suddenly from the doorway and, as she turned her aching head, he was there, his eyes full of anguished concern.

'Ben,' she said faintly. 'I got hit.'

He came striding across and took her hand and she could feel the cold fury in him.

'You most certainly did,' he groaned as he inspected her face. 'I can't take my eyes off you for one second. That oaf Walsh wants locking up!'

'It's one of the hazards of the job, Ben,' she said weakly. 'We all know that, and please, don't start ticking me off again, or I shall start blubbering like a baby.'

'I'm not going to, my poor battered love,' he said gently, and to the doctor who was patiently waiting to get a word in, 'I have my car outside. Once you've stitched the cut I'll take her home and, needless to say, I won't take my eyes off the lady.'

'That's fine, then,' the other man said.

As Tessa sat huddled in Ben's car once more, she became aware that they weren't heading for the flat.

'Where are you taking me?' she asked through painful lips.

'Where do you expect?' he asked, in the same gentle tones that he'd used at the hospital. 'I'm taking you to the farm.'

'But you can't do that,' she protested weakly. 'What about all your Christmas arrangements?'

'What about yours?' he parried.

There was no point in beating about the bush.

'I didn't have any.'

He smiled.

'Neither did I.'

So they would each have been spending Christmas alone, she thought in amazement. Maybe the aggressive Jack Walsh was another gift from Santa.

When they got to the farm it was a cold clear night again, and the snow was still there, glistening whitely under a pale moon. If she'd been in a less fragile state Tessa might have expected to hear sleigh-bells but, as it was, she just wanted to lie down and forget her hurts.

Yet they were only physical, weren't they? Her mental hurt had vanished as if it had never existed when Ben had called her his love, and now he'd brought her to his home to look after her, and in her wildest dreams she'd never expected that.

'Stay where you are,' he commanded as he switched off the engine. 'Once I've unlocked the door I'll come back for you,' and in her present painful state she didn't argue.

When he swung her up in his arms she nestled her cheek against his shoulder, and then moved it away with a smothered groan as pain shot through her face. Ben glanced down at her, the anxiety still there in his eyes, and then he carried her up the stairs and into his room, and laid her gently on the bed.

As she lay there limply, looking up at him, he said, 'You may be in no fit state to hear this, but I'm going to tell you now what I should have told you ages ago. I love you, Tessa Martin, and the only reason I've gone off at the deep end sometimes is because it's been hard trying to put you out of my mind, when everywhere I've turned you've been there distracting me.

'I'm older than you, and never in a thousand years did I expect to fall in love with a cocky brown-haired youngster, who blithely told me that she was expecting my chosen profession to be a piece of cake. But, you see, I discovered that she was warm and generous, and very beautiful in her own special way, in spite of there being times when she was a one-woman disaster area!'

'I think I *must* have concussion,' she told him tremulously, 'because I thought I heard you say that you loved me.'

'I'll say it again, if you like.'

'Yes, please.'

'I love you, Tess,' he said tenderly. 'You make me laugh, you make me feel young, and you make me feel proud.'

'Proud?'

'Yes, because you're going to make a damned good GP, and if Hugo keeps to his word and finishes soon, there is no place where I'd rather see you practise than at Woodbank.'

'You really think so?'

'Do I ever say things I don't mean?'

'Not often,' she said, with an attempt at a stiff smile. 'But what about Georgina?'

'What about her?' he said impatiently. 'I can't ever remember telling you that she meant anything to me now. I did care for her once, a long time ago, but I hadn't thought of her in years until she reappeared on the scene, and any time I've spent with her is because she is very traumatised over the death of her husband, and I've been trying to talk her through it.'

'And Anne-Marie?'

'She's just had a good ticking-off and been told to watch her step. She knows what Jack Walsh is like, and yet she let him go through to you without any warning.'

'I can forgive her. I can forgive him. I can forgive

everybody and everything. . .because you love me,' she told him, with joy in her voice.

'I'm not sure I can say the same,' he said soberly. 'Between her conniving, and his temper, you could have been killed, and that would have finished me off, too.'

'Don't, Ben,' she pleaded. 'Let's start off without any rancour in our hearts.'

He was still unconvinced.

'The police will be wanting to talk to you,' he pointed out. 'They'll be asking if you want to press charges.'

'I don't,' she said firmly. 'That really would ruin the Walshes' marriage, but I'd like to know what it was all about.'

'Jack has been rough with his wife once or twice when he's been drinking, even though he dotes on her when he's sober, and either she's been leading him on, or he'd got the wrong end of the stick, I don't know. Anyway, he came lusting for revenge because he thought I'd told her to leave him, when the truth of the matter is that my only involvement was to give her the name of a refuge when she asked for one.

'It seems that she used the information rather mischievously by leaving him a note to say that she and the children had gone into the refuge that I'd recommended. She knew he would be coming home drunk and thought it would teach him a lesson, when actually she'd merely taken the family Christmas shopping. We know the rest, don't we? Instead of Jack taking it out on me—or her—he came and attacked a defenceless young girl.'

'Not so defenceless!' she protested. 'It was just that he wasn't in the right position for me to get an arm-lock on him.'

'That's it, you see,' he said quizzically. 'I have no

choice but to marry you. It's the only way to keep you under control. From the moment I met you again, I've been in a state of dread in case anything happened to take you away from me. Now, as I can't kiss you, I'm going to bring us up some supper, and then I'll tuck you up for the night either in here or in the guest room, whichever you prefer.'

'In here, please,' she said, snuggling against the pillows, and with an attempt at a smile, 'and if you wouldn't think it improper I'd like you beside me, as the doctor in Casualty said I have to be watched over.'

'I have every intention of doing that,' he told her, teasing one of her dreadlocks with a gentle finger. 'In fact, I intend to watch over you for the rest of your life.'

'That is what I want, Ben,' she said softly, 'and I don't think it will hurt *too* much if you kiss me.'

When Tessa awoke on Christmas morning she found Ben lying on top of the covers beside her, fully clothed, with his hair tousled, fair stubble on his chin, and one arm flung protectively across her.

As she turned her head to absorb the exquisite pleasure of his presence, the bruising of her face brought forth a soft gasp of pain, and immediately he was awake, his eyes raking her face for any signs of distress.

'I'm all right,' she said softly. 'Just sore and puffy. I must look dreadful.'

He was eyeing her sleepily.

'You certainly wouldn't win any prizes in a beauty competition at the moment, my love,' he said with a grin, 'but as you're always telling me, it's what we are inside that counts.'

Tessa traced her finger gently against his bristly cheek.

'I still can't believe that you love me.'

He reached across to where a small pile of gifts on the bedside table was waiting to be opened, and taking the smallest one off the top he handed it to her.

'All those are for you,' he said gravely, 'but this is the one that tells you why you should believe it. Open it, Tessa.'

She turned the small gift-wrapped box over in her hand and looked up at him.

'You've bought me all those things and I've only bought you a sweater, and I wasn't even sure I'd have the nerve to give it to you.'

'Your being here with me is the best gift of all,' he said, 'and if you accept what is in the box my life will be complete.'

When she opened the package she found a gold ring with a glowing emerald in the centre, shining up at her from out of a small velvet box and, her eyes huge with wonder, she asked, 'Is this the ring that you had made, and they lost it in the shop?'

'The very same. So you can see how important it was for them to find it, and why I wouldn't leave the place until they did.' He kissed her swollen lips gently. 'Are we going to put it on?'

'Yes, please,' she whispered.

'It should fit,' he told her, as he slid it gently on to her slender finger, 'as I had it made to your size.'

'How did you manage that?' she asked curiously.

He pointed to the little gold signet ring that she'd always worn on that finger.

'You left that in the kitchen one day after you'd washed your hands, and I took a quick measurement.'

'So you were *that* sure of me, Ben? And I thought I was hiding my passion for you so well.'

'It was only myself that I was sure of,' he told her tenderly, 'and the knowledge that if I let you slip away from me, I would. . .'

'Spend a lifetime of regret,' they chorused with shared laughter.

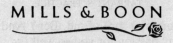

GET 4 BOOKS
AND A MYSTERY GIFT

Return this coupon and we'll send you 4 Love on Call novels and a mystery gift absolutely FREE! We'll even pay the postage and packing for you.

We're making you this offer to introduce you to the benefits of Reader Service: FREE home delivery of brand-new Love on Call novels, at least a month before they are available in the shops, FREE gifts and a monthly Newsletter packed with information.

Accepting these FREE books and gift places you under no obligation to buy, you may cancel at any time, even after receiving just your free shipment. Simply complete the coupon below and send it to:

HARLEQUIN MILLS & BOON, FREEPOST, PO BOX 70, CROYDON, CR9 9EL.

No stamp needed

Yes, please send me 4 free Love on Call novels and a mystery gift. I understand that unless you hear from me, I will receive 4 superb new titles every month for just £1.99* each postage and packing free. I am under no obligation to purchase any books and I may cancel or suspend my subscription at any time, but the free books and gifts will be mine to keep in any case. (I am over 18 years of age)

2EP5D

Ms/Mrs/Miss/Mr _____

Address _____

_____

_____ Postcode _____

Offer closes 31st January 1996. We reserve the right to refuse an application. *Prices and terms subject to change without notice. Offer only valid in UK and Ireland and is not available to current subscribers to this series. **Readers in Ireland please write to: P.O. Box 4546, Dublin 24.** Overseas readers please write for details.

You may be mailed with offers from other reputable companies as a result of this application. Please tick box if you would prefer not to receive such offers.

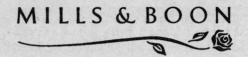

MILLS & BOON

LOVE ON CALL

The books for enjoyment this month are:

LOVE WITHOUT MEASURE   Caroline Anderson
VERSATILE VET   Mary Bowring
TARRANT'S PRACTICE   Abigail Gordon
DOCTOR'S HONOUR   Marion Lennox

Treats in store!

Watch next month for the following absorbing stories:

MIDWIFE'S DILEMMA   Lilian Darcy
MADE FOR EACH OTHER   Elizabeth Harrison
HOSPITAL AT RISK   Clare Lavenham
SEEING EYE TO EYE   Josie Metcalfe

Available from W.H. Smith, John Menzies, Volume One, Forbuoys,
Martins, Tesco, Asda, Safeway and other paperback stockists.

Readers in South Africa - write to:
IBS, Private Bag X3010, Randburg 2125.